MT. PLEASANT

VAI W9-AQT-602

THE
DEVOURING WOLF

THE DEVOURING WOLF

NATALIE C. PARKER

RAZORBILL

RAZORBILL

An imprint of Penguin Random House LLC, New York

First published in the United States of America by Razorbill,
an imprint of Penguin Random House LLC, 2022

Text copyright © 2022 by Natalie C. Parker
Interior illustrations copyright © 2022 by Tyler Champion

Penguin supports copyright. Copyright fuels creativity, encourages diverse voices, promotes free speech, and creates a vibrant culture. Thank you for buying an authorized edition of this book and for complying with copyright laws by not reproducing, scanning, or distributing any part of it in any form without permission. You are supporting writers and allowing Penguin to continue to publish books for every reader.

Razorbill & colophon are registered trademarks of Penguin Random House LLC.

Visit us online at penguinrandomhouse.com.

LIBRARY OF CONGRESS CATALOGING-IN-PUBLICATION DATA
Names: Parker, Natalie C., author.
Title: The Devouring Wolf / Natalie C. Parker.
Description: New York : Razorbill, 2022. | Audience: Ages 8–12 years. |
Summary: To find out why twelve-year-old Riley and the rest of the
sapling pack did not transform into werewolves on the first full moon
of the summer, they must unearth their community's deepest
secrets and face a terrifying legendary creature.
Identifiers: LCCN 2022011396 | ISBN 9780593203958 (hardcover) | ISBN
9780593203972 (trade paperback) | ISBN 9780593203965 (ebook)
Subjects: CYAC: Werewolves—Fiction. | LGBTQ+ people—Fiction. |
LCGFT: Werewolf fiction. | Novels.
Classification: LCC PZ7.P2275 De 2022 | DDC [Fic]—dc23
LC record available at https://lccn.loc.gov/2022011396

Manufactured in Canada

1 3 5 7 9 10 8 6 4 2

FRI

Design by Tony Sahara
Text set in Averia Serif Libre Light

This book is a work of fiction. Any references to historical events, real people, or real places are used fictitiously. Other names, characters, places, and events are products of the author's imagination, and any resemblance to actual events or places or persons, living or dead, is entirely coincidental.

The publisher does not have any control over and does not assume any responsibility for author or third-party websites or their content.

For my mom,
who taught me to howl at the moon

PROLOGUE

THE SOUTH WOOD

The air was eerily silent as a wolf cut a silky path through the thick summertime growth of the woods. She moved as if on a mission, sweeping her gaze across old oak trees and silver maples, eyes and ears alert. A rabbit froze beneath a coil of honeysuckle vines. Its small body went still as the wolf came near. The wolf felt its little muscles tense. But she passed the rabbit without a second glance, senses trained on what lay just ahead.

Something was wrong, something was very wrong, but the wolf didn't know what. It was a feeling in her chest, drawing her forward like magic. But she knew magic, and she did not know this feeling.

The wolf should have been the most dangerous thing in the woods that day. But she wasn't.

In the distance, she could sense the other four members of her prime pack. They were spread out through the South Wood, their minds linked just enough to sense one another as they searched for anything that shouldn't be there.

That tugging sensation pulled again, this time strong enough to make the wolf stumble into a quiet grove surrounded by thorny honey locust trees. It was a place she had never seen before. In the center of the grove stood a large stone. It was stormy gray, much darker than the flinty stones peppered throughout the Kansas prairie, and it glittered in the sunlight as though webbed with crystals. It was old and heavy, but completely unfamiliar to the wolf, which in itself was cause for alarm.

The pack had lived on these lands for generations. How could something like this go unnoticed for so long?

The wolf tipped her head to consider the stone. Then she came forward slowly. The fur along her spine rose and her snout tickled in the way it always did when danger was near. She sniffed at the air, but there was no sign of hunters or witches. At least, none that she recognized. She crept closer, but before she reached the stone, she paused.

She lowered her head and closed her eyes, drawing a deep breath into her lungs. A shiver moved from the crown of her head all the way down to her toes. She followed the feeling, reaching her forelegs out in front and pushing her hips up high as the transformation rippled through her body. Her paws stretched into long fingers, her snout shortened into a nose that bent slightly to the left, her fur faded against her skin, until it wasn't a wolf standing in the clearing anymore. It was a woman.

Loose pants hung from her hips, and the green shirt she wore was battered along the hem. She pressed one hand against her chest, rubbing over the place where she still felt that strange, uncomfortable tugging. Then she stepped toward the stone on bare feet.

In all her years patrolling the South Wood, she had never seen anything like this stone. It radiated energy, sending out magical probes like fishing hooks. Like the one lodged in her chest. And it had hooked her when she was nearly a quarter mile away.

She decided to push back, just a little, to see what it would do. Squaring her shoulders, she began to howl. She chose a note that would push gently at the stone's exterior, the same note she'd use to nudge the refrigerator door shut when someone in her house inevitably left it open. A small test, so she was surprised when her howl snapped back toward her as though it had encountered something electric.

Whatever this stone was, it was powerful. It was wolf magic.

She should leave and return with her prime pack. She could still feel them. All four were close enough that she could reach them quickly. Crow was the closest, paused along the southern bend of Blood Creek. But the hook in her chest tugged a little harder, drew her a few steps nearer.

Before she knew what she was doing, the woman had

raised a hand and pressed it flat against the stone. She could not resist. She felt the rough warmth of it against her palm. And suddenly, she had the sense that she had made a grave mistake.

She tried to pull her hand back, but it was stuck. It was as if her skin had fused with the stone. She pulled again but with no luck. On her third tug, the stone pulled back and her hand began sinking inside it, fingers disappearing under the surface, becoming heavy and still as they vanished inside the rock. Panic shot through her lungs.

"Help!" she called. Then, thinking of her pack, she began to howl. Crow was near enough to help. She only had to reach him. But the sound was cut off, muffled and muted by the magic encasing the stone.

She cried out again, but her voice faded as she heard a growl like the lowest rumble of thunder. It was a warning from a stranger, and it sent a shiver of fear down her spine.

"Your wolf is mine," the thunderous voice said.

She spun around, as best she could with her arm sinking into the rock, but saw no one. No wolf. No movement.

She couldn't even sense her pack anymore. She was completely cut off. Completely alone.

She tugged again. This time, she braced a foot against the stone and pulled as hard as she could, hard enough that she thought she might tear her own skin. But it was no use. No matter how hard she fought, the stone kept pulling.

And pulling.

Until the woman could move only her eyes, her mouth, and nothing else. She was surrounded by stone, sinking inside it as though it were an ocean and she were nothing more than a shell.

"Please—" she gasped as the stone filled her mouth.

There were tears in her eyes now. She blinked them away, still fighting, still furious and afraid. Someone would find her. Someone would come looking for her when she didn't return. Her pack, her family would come for her.

As the stone closed over her face and eyes, she caught a final glimpse of the world beyond. Someone was there. Standing in front of the stone. Looking at her with a smile on their familiar face, and she realized with a cold kind of certainty that just as the stone had drawn her inside, it had let someone else out.

My friends,

We don't know each other, but if this diary has found you, then the unthinkable has happened and he has returned. I have enspelled this diary to reveal itself only to you. It is the only way I know to help. I wish I could do more.

Be vigilant. Be strong. And most of all, stay together. You will need each other more than you can imagine.

With greatest love,
Grace Barley

ROCK, PAPER, SQUISHERS

All her life, Riley Callahan had been looking forward to becoming a real wolf.

Both of her moms were werewolves, and that meant that sometime between the ages of nine and twelve, on the night of the first full moon of summer, Riley would also become one. And she'd been counting down the days, nights, and in-between times for years.

Her older sister, Darcy, had turned when she was ten. She'd been a werewolf six whole years already, running with her prime pack out at Wax & Wayne, the hills and valleys and forests just outside Lawrence, Kansas, where wolves could run safely. Riley had hoped she would also turn when she was ten, but it hadn't happened.

It also hadn't happened last year when her best friend, Stacey, turned at age eleven. Riley had been so sure they would turn together. They did everything else together—

it only made sense that they would become wolves at the same time. But Stacey had turned and Riley had not, which officially made Riley the last one of their small group of friends who was still trapped in her bipedal form. But that was about to change, because this year she was twelve years old, and tonight was the first full moon of summer. In a few torturously long hours, she would finally, finally become a werewolf.

In the meantime, she was in the backyard with her little brother, Milo, trying to hide grapes inside of rocks. It required a combination of two of the three forms of wolf magic: alchemy, or the magic of transformation, and lithomancy, the magic of stones. It also required practice.

"Is this really the kind of stuff they teach at Tenderfoot Camp?" Milo asked as another grape made a small popping noise before disintegrating in his hands. He groaned, letting the pulp slip off his fingers into an already-gushy pile of mashed fruit. "I thought we'd be doing cool stuff like playing hide-and-call or learning how to turn sticks into fire or something. Why would I ever need to put grapes inside rocks?"

Riley glared at the mess before her. Instead of a mountainous, gloopy mush, like Milo, Riley had a sticky pile of rocks. No matter what she did, the stones kept crushing the grapes.

"You don't turn sticks into fire, you ignite them with alchemy. And they don't teach this exactly," Riley explained. Having attended Tenderfoot Camp for the past three summers, she knew the curriculum inside and out. "This is just extra practice."

The real reason was that magic like this, blending one kind with another, was advanced. It was hard to master, and Riley wanted to be very good at doing difficult magic. Like her mom, Cecelia Callahan.

Mama C had started blending magic before her first transformation, and the way Mama N told it, the entire pack had been impressed. They knew from that moment on that Cecelia Callahan was destined to become a pack alpha. Riley loved that story. She loved the way Mama N's face lit up when she told it and the way Mama C blushed. It was part of what made her special.

Riley wanted people to talk about her that way one day. She wanted to make her moms proud of her and become an alpha. She wanted to be so important to her pack that they would never think about leaving her. But Milo didn't need to know all that.

"Just think, if you get good at it, then you can hide better things inside them, like chocolates or jelly beans or maybe even cookies."

"Why would I want to put any of those things inside rocks? Why wouldn't I just eat them? Wait." Milo screwed up his mouth and tilted his head, hazel eyes peering out from beneath a mop of curly brown hair. "Do you have cookies?"

In many ways, Milo was Riley's mirror. They both had wintery-white skin and dark brown hair, with eyes Mama N called mosaic green, and they both had a major weakness for cookies.

Even though they were seated in the shade of the big oak tree in their backyard, the Kansas sun drew heat around them like a heavy cloak. Riley wiped at the sweat on her forehead.

"No, I don't have cookies. But think about it. You could hide candy in your bedroom in plain sight."

"Oooh!" Milo swiped a handful of grapes and melted onto his back. "I wish the sun would hurry up and set already. Why does all the cool magic stuff have to happen at night?!"

Ignoring her brother, Riley selected a dusty piece of sandstone and held it next to a purple grape. She took a deep breath and concentrated, letting her magic unfurl inside of her the way she'd been taught. The stone shivered and warmed against her skin. The grape began to slide through the stone, but just as it was about to disappear inside it, juice dribbled out of the stone.

"Rock, paper, squishers." Riley threw her wet rock onto the growing pile with disappointment.

"Still working on the stone case?" Darcy called,

emerging from the house through the sliding glass door.

"And failing," Milo called, tossing a grape at Riley's head.

Darcy laughed, crossing the yard toward them. She'd grown several inches since winter, and her body had slimmed down and sprouted new angles all at once. Her white skin was already honeyed by the summer sun and her features were petite like Mama N's, all except for her eyes, which were big and brown. Today she wore a trans pride T-shirt and cutoff jean shorts.

"It's like this." Darcy knelt on the ground between them, reaching for a stone and a grape. She held them in her open palm and smiled. "Remember to imagine the room inside the stone before you draw them together."

That was exactly how Mama C described it, too. Like it was just that easy.

Riley nodded and watched as Darcy's grape moved seamlessly inside the stone. Not a drop of pulp or juice was left behind. She tossed it to Riley.

"Why don't you try separating them again? Sometimes that's easier."

The stone was still warm from the magic. Other than that, it was several layers of tan and brown all squished together just like any other piece of Kansas sandstone. There was no sign of the fruit it now concealed.

Riley cupped it in her hand and pictured the room inside the stone with a grape in it. Then she started to draw the fruit out. Magic tingled against her skin. She thought it was working until—*squish.* Juice coated her palm.

"Why can't I get this? I don't understand!" Riley threw the rock down in frustration and slapped her palms to her forehead before she remembered the sticky juice all over them. "Oh, great."

She peeled her fingers away, but it was too late. She'd painted her face with bits of grape pulp.

"Hey, hey, Lilee," Darcy said, using the name Milo had given her when he was too young to pronounce his *r*'s. "You're always taking these things too seriously. There's no rush. Learning wolf magic isn't a race, it's—"

"A journey we take at our own speed," the three of them sang together. It was something Mama N said nearly every day. Most often to Riley.

But even though Riley knew it was true, she worried that she was too slow.

"Right, and some things just get easier when you're a wolf," Darcy added.

When you're a wolf.

The words stirred something uncomfortable and excited in Riley at the same time. For the past three years, she'd waited and hoped that it would be her turn, that she would finally be a real wolf, and every year, she'd struggled to hide her disappointment when it didn't happen. It had been especially hard last year when Stacey turned and Riley spent most of the summer trying not to die of jealousy. It was hard to watch everyone else growing up so much faster, finding their prime packs and doing things only real wolves could do. Things Riley couldn't.

After tonight, no one would say things like "when you're a wolf" to her ever again. She just had to be patient.

Riley forced a smile and nodded. "I know you're right."

"I'm about to go join my prime, but I'll be out there tonight. Me and Mama C and Aunt Alexis, we'll all be there, ready to run with you." Darcy put a hand on Riley's shoulder and gave a light squeeze. "I just wanted to wish you both good luck and swift feet before I left."

Warmth spread through Riley's cheeks and down into her chest. Tonight she would run with her family as the daughter of Great Pack Leader Callahan. She was so eager to stand next to Mama C as a wolf, she almost couldn't speak.

"Thanks," Riley managed.

Milo, however, threw a grape a Darcy's head and howled in delighted surprise when Darcy expertly caught it in her mouth and chewed gleefully.

"I'm super glad that wasn't a rock." Darcy climbed to her feet and waved. "See ya, pups!"

"It didn't even occur to me to throw a rock!" Milo threw his hands into the air as though this were a great tragedy. "Next time," he promised. "Wanna try again?"

Riley tugged her phone from her pocket and tapped the screen. It had been exactly forty-three minutes since Riley sent the text, and there was still no response from Stacey. Not that *Eeeeeee!* really demanded a response, but ever since Stacey had found her own prime pack, she'd been a little more distant.

With a sigh, Riley looked back at the piles of rocks and grapes. Maybe things would get easier when she was a real wolf. Maybe they wouldn't. Maybe all she needed was a little more practice.

"Yeah," she said, taking a fresh grape in hand.

This time when she reached for her magic, she was patient. She imagined that the room inside the stone was shaped exactly like the fruit. When she was sure she was ready, she pictured the grape inside the room. A perfect fit meant only for that specific gra—

A subtle chill landed on her shoulders and a low, ominous growl sounded in her ears.

She froze. Shivers skittered down her spine. Then she felt it. Hot breath on her neck as the growl rumbled again.

She struggled to swallow, too terrified to move. She was aware that Milo was right in front of her, all his attention focused on his rock. Didn't he see whoever was behind her?

Little wolf, little wolf, here I come.

Riley snapped around. The words had been a whisper in her ear. The voice strange and threatening.

But the yard behind her was empty. Nothing, no one, was there.

"Uuugh," Milo groaned.

Feeling uncertain, Riley turned to face her brother.

"Squishers," he said, holding up his hand as evidence.

"Did you hear that?" Riley asked in a thin voice.

"Hear what? Hey! Did you do it?!"

"What?" Riley looked down to find the stone in her hand was perfectly dry, the grape safely inside it. "I—I guess."

"That's so cool!" Milo crowed. "Can I have it? Wait, I'm gonna show Mama N."

Stone in hand, Milo hopped up and ran toward the house as though nothing strange had happened.

Whatever had spoken in Riley's ear, Milo hadn't seen a thing.

2

THE FIRST FULL MOON
OF SUMMER

"Mom!" Riley rushed through the sliding glass doors and past the kitchen table and swung around the corner to pound up the stairs. "Mom!"

She shot past Milo's room, where the sound of a vacuum cleaner roared behind a closed door, then past Darcy's, which was perfectly in order and empty, and was about to fly past her own when she spotted Mama N out of the corner of her eye, standing by Riley's unmade bed.

"Mom!" Riley hopped over the pile of dirty clothes blocking her doorway. "Mom, I have to tell you something!"

"Is it that you're going to clean up this room right this second? Or that you've already cleaned out the cat litter boxes? Or that you've done any of the other chores I've already asked you to do twice?" Mama N raised an eyebrow and tipped her head to one side. Waiting.

Mama N was the kind of person who always looked like they were on the very brink of chaos. Or like they'd just come through a tornado—if that tornado were filled with a bunch of wet paints, an assortment of yoga pants, and black combat boots. She was short and slim with dark brown eyes that didn't miss a thing, and she always had a few smudges of paint on her cheeks. Today they were lavender and navy blue, like a twilight sky or a bruise.

"Um, no, but—"

"Riley, it is already five o'clock. I need you and your brother to stop getting distracted and get your chores done." Mama N turned to the bed and started to strip the sheets.

"I will, I will, but I need to tell you something." Mama N paused, giving Riley her full attention. "When Milo and I were outside just now, I heard a growling noise and a whisper. Like someone was in our backyard, but Milo didn't hear anything."

Now that she'd said it aloud, it sounded ridiculous. Judging by the exasperation on Mama N's face, she thought so, too.

"Are you sure it wasn't something that just sounded like a growl?" Mama N asked.

"I don't think so. It felt real. In a wolf way."

"Then it probably has something to do with the full moon." Mama N resumed bundling Riley's sheets. "Your magic is restless because it knows you're finally becoming a wolf tonight."

Riley didn't like the word *finally*. It was true, and Mama N didn't mean it in a bad way, but it made her feel like she was late to the party. Like she'd been dragging her feet for the past three years. Which was as far from the truth as it could possibly be.

"It's natural for you to feel a little different right now. Okay?"

"Okay," Riley muttered, but she wished Mama C were here to ask instead.

Mama C had all kinds of responsibilities and often had to leave in the middle of dinner or very early in the morning to go take care of wolf business. This morning, she had risen before the sun and slipped into Riley's room to plant a kiss on her forehead. Riley had a dim memory of hearing Mama C say something like "I'll see you tonight, pup. I'm so proud of you." Remembering it now filled Riley with a rush of excitement. Tonight, she would run with her mom and her sister under the light of the first full moon of summer. It wasn't that Mama N didn't care, but she wasn't a born wolf. She didn't *really* know what it was like to transform at the Full Moon Rite because she'd never done it.

Mama N paused at the door. "Oh, also, I forgot to tell you that Uncle Will is going to come take you to Wax & Wayne tonight."

"Just me? Why?"

"Because it's Milo's first year; it's a special time for him," Mama N explained. "I need to get him all set up for camp in case he doesn't transform. You remember."

Riley did remember. She remembered the past three Full Moon Rites in excruciating detail. She'd gone to each one hoping that she would transform, only to be disappointed. One by one, each of her closest friends had transformed, leaving her further and further behind.

This year *was* a special year for Milo. But it was special for Riley, too. It was finally, finally her turn, and she'd assumed they'd drive out together like they always had.

"But why can't I go out early, too?" Riley asked, trying not to sound as pitiful as she felt.

She didn't mind riding with Uncle Will and her cousin Dhonielle on principle. They were her family, after all. But once again, she was being left behind.

"Oh, you'd just be bored. Besides, this way, you get to go with your cousin." Mama N flashed a big smile, then looked pointedly around the room. "You have one hour till dinner."

There was no use in arguing. When Mama N made up her mind about something, it was nearly impossible to change. Especially when it came to Milo. He was always getting away with things Riley couldn't, like only eating half of his brussels sprouts at dinner or staying up after bedtime to watch the end of a movie. Things she never would have been allowed to do when she was nine.

Riley swallowed hard and told herself it didn't matter because after tonight, she'd be a wolf. A real wolf. She'd run with the other young wolves for a month while her magic settled into her body, and she would find her prime pack. Five wolves linked by magic. Five wolves who would come together during the first transformation. Five wolves who would protect and love each other for the rest of their lives. Five wolves who would never leave her behind on the most important night of her life.

Riley looked around her room. It was, as usual, a perfect disaster. Clothes were strewn across the floor, there were colored pencils spilled in one corner, and her walls were dotted with hastily tacked-up drawings. Only the ones she was most proud of made it to the wall. The rest were tossed around the room in crumpled balls. Without wolf magic, it would take ages to clean everything.

With a clap of her hands, Riley reached for her magic and stirred a wind. It raced around her room, kicking up the clothes like autumn leaves. This was an alchemy trick she'd learned at Tenderfoot Camp last year. On its own, it wasn't very useful for cleaning, but Riley had figured out that she could direct the wind with the third form of wolf magic: acoustics or howling magic. Riley aimed her howl at shirts and pants, socks and swimsuits, tossing them toward the laundry basket like a pro.

She was just wrapping up the last of her chores when Mama N shouted that the pizza had arrived and it was time for dinner. Milo's choice, of course. Riley would have chosen fajitas, but the youngest tenderfoot always got to choose the meal on the first full moon of summer. Riley knew she shouldn't mind. But it was hard to ignore the fact that Mama N only seemed to care that tonight was special for Milo.

"Uuugh, I wanted pepperoni, pineapple, and olives!" Milo whined, searching through both boxes for his missing olives.

"Oh, they must have forgotten." Immediately, Mama N hopped up from her seat. "That's okay. We've got a can of olives in the pantry. I just have to slice them up."

"It's not the same," Milo muttered, pouting at his pizza as though the lack of olives was ruining everything.

Not only was Milo fussing about something as inconsequential as olives, but there was a decent chance he might transform tonight, too. The injustice of it all was starting to irritate Riley. And when Riley got irritated, Riley got even.

"You know," Riley said in a low voice, quickly settling on scary stories as the best means of retaliation. None was better than the oldest wolf legend she knew. "They say that the Devouring Wolf always prowls on the night of the first full moon of summer."

Milo froze with a slice of pizza halfway to his mouth.

"Who—who's that?" he finally asked.

"You haven't heard of him yet?" Riley leaned in,

conspiratorial and careful to speak so Mama N couldn't hear. "They say he's like a ghost and he's just waiting for the perfect pup to come along so he can steal their wolf away and keep it for himself."

"He can steal wolves?" Milo's voice was barely a whisper, his pizza forgotten in his hand.

"Yup." Riley nodded confidently, emboldened by the fear in her little brother's eyes. "Rips them right out of you! But it helps if you aren't very strong yet. That's why he prowls the woods tonight. When the new wolves are too confused to know the difference between him and their pack."

Milo's eyes darted toward the kitchen, but their mom was still chopping olives.

"You're making it up," he said, but he didn't sound convinced.

"No, I'm not." Riley reached for her own pizza to hide a smile. She was too old to believe in the Devouring Wolf anymore, but Milo was only nine. He'd believe almost anything if she told it right. "I heard that he has to steal a new wolf every ten years. And the last time he took one was . . ." Riley pretended to think for a minute. "Exactly ten years ago. He must be hungry again."

"Mom!" Milo shrieked.

"Riley, stop teasing your brother!" It didn't matter that she hadn't heard a word of the exchange; she believed the accusation in Milo's voice.

Riley glowered as Mama N appeared holding a bowl of sliced olives.

"Eat up, pups! Milo and I have to go in fifteen minutes."

Those minutes flew by, and before Riley knew it, Mama N was boxing up the leftovers.

As Milo ran to get his things, Mama N came around the table and caught Riley's face in her hands. She planted a kiss on each cheek like always and then smiled. "I'm so happy for you, Riley. You're going to make an incredible wolf. I'll see you out there. Okay?"

"Okay." Riley took her empty plate to the kitchen, then watched them load Milo's luggage and sleeping bag into Mama N's red Prius. The tenderfoot pups who didn't transform during the Full Moon Rite, along with the pups who had turned in previous years, would all stay on the grounds of Wax & Wayne for Tenderfoot Camp. Only those who transformed for the first time tonight would run with the pack.

Before Riley knew it, Mama N and Milo were driving away, leaving her alone in the house. She was used to being home alone. Now that she was twelve, she was allowed to do things like babysit Milo and stay home by herself for a few hours, but without Milo roaring around or Mama N shouting final instructions, the house felt too big and too quiet. Unless Riley moved, it was nearly silent, except for the occasional groan of wood, the tick of the air conditioner, and a faint whine coming up from the basement that sounded a little too much like a ghost.

It reminded her of the growl in the backyard, the hot breath on her neck, the Devouring Wolf skulking through the woods, and suddenly Riley deeply regretted her decision to tell Milo ghost stories about wolves.

Her heart was pounding in her ears and she was genuinely starting to freak out. To keep herself calm, she recalled Rule #1 of Cecelia Callahan's Alpha Code, *Don't panic, plan it,* and tried to focus on her pre–Full Moon Rite plan. It had three steps.

The first was to eat a big dinner. Which she'd done.

The second was to dress in natural fibers. Clothing didn't always survive the first transformation, but it was more likely if the fibers weren't made of plastic or polyester.

The third step was to leave absolutely everything else behind. Every other year, Riley had taken all her camp stuff with her: an entire duffel of clothing, a sleeping bag, and a pillow, to be exact. But Riley had attended camp three years in a row. She was done with it. This year all she needed to do was show up.

At the hall tree by the front door, Riley hung her house keys on the key rack, then set her phone on the wireless charging station. After tonight, she wouldn't need either for a month, and it was unlikely they would survive her first transformation anyway.

In the mirror, Riley caught a glimpse of her reflection—hair one shade lighter than black; mosaic-green eyes; a cool, moonish complexion; and not a freckle in sight. She looked like she had every other day this summer: a twelve-year-old tenderfoot on the brink of becoming a full werewolf.

She grinned wolfishly at herself and wondered what she would look like after.

The house groaned again. Riley squeezed her hands into tight fists. It was not a growl. It only sounded like one. A lot like one.

By the time Uncle Will's sleek gray minivan pulled into the driveway, Riley was so anxious that she exploded through the front door.

"Happy Moon Rite, Riley," Uncle Will called as she raced to the van.

Uncle Will was a tall Black man with long locs that were starting to go silver at the roots. He was originally from the packs in southern Mississippi, but the way Riley had heard it, he'd come to Kansas for college, fallen in love with Aunt Alexis, and stayed put. Now, when he wasn't busy being a werewolf, he sold books at the Raven Book Store in downtown Lawrence.

"Thanks," Riley called back.

"All ready to go?"

"Yeah," she confirmed, trying not to shudder. "Very ready."

"Hey, Riley," a small voice said from within the van.

Dhonielle was seated in one of the two middle seats. Unlike Riley, she was narrow and sort of wiry, her shoulders almost always hunched up toward her ears like she was waiting for something to explode. She had big eyes that were the same soft tan as an oak and skin that was a warm copper brown. Her dark hair was twisted into two braids down either side of her head. She reminded Riley of a little bird, blinking and afraid of almost everything.

Riley liked Dhonielle. They'd always gotten along, but they weren't friends the way she and Stacey were friends. Mostly because Dhonielle was scared of her own shadow and Riley would be first in line to meet a ghost.

"Happy Moon Rite, Dhonielle," Riley said.

Dhonielle was also twelve, one of a handful of others who were still waiting for their first transformation. It was possible the two of them would end up in the same prime pack, which would be fine with Riley. If she ended up in a pack with Dhonielle, there would be one less person competing with her to be alpha.

"You can sit here, if you want," Dhonielle offered shyly, gesturing to the seat next to her.

"You know you can't take that with you, right?" Riley pointed at the book in Dhonielle's hands as she climbed into the seat and buckled up.

But Dhonielle nodded seriously. "I know. A *month*

without any reading. I don't even know how I'm going to manage it. I gotta read as many words as I can before we get there."

Riley shook her head. She couldn't imagine reading on a night like tonight.

"Everyone buckled?" Uncle Will called. When he landed behind the wheel, the whole van bounced with him.

"Yep," Dhonielle chirped.

As they pulled out of the driveway and onto the road, Riley turned for one last look at her house. The turn-of-the-century bungalow was surrounded by early summer flowers, the front porch was cast in shadow, but the roof was gilded in a bright, fiery orange as the sun set behind it. There was Cottonwood, one of her four cats, perched atop the roof, and down below was her bicycle, leaned against the side gate.

It seemed silly now to have worried about that growl. Her house was exactly as it should be, and her mom was probably right. It was something to do with the full moon and her magic finally starting to mature. Something to do with the fact that she was about to become a real wolf. Nothing more.

At least, that is what she hoped.

It's important that you know how this happened. How he happened. He wasn't a bad person. He wasn't evil in the beginning, just a person bad things happened to. So many bad things that it ate up all the good inside him.

It started with the tragic death of his family. We had no idea the hunters had come so close to our village. If the greats had known, they never would have let us roam the woods as wolves. But they didn't know, and one day his wife and child were caught in a hunters' snare more powerful than any we'd ever seen. Not even magic could save them. In the course of a swift and vicious hour, he lost nearly everything he'd ever loved.

But in the course of a week, he took so much more.

3

WAX & WAYNE

Instead of reading, Dhonielle spent the whole drive snapping her book shut to ask her dad nervous questions about what the transformation was going to feel like. Riley knew how it was going to feel. It was going to feel amazing. And she didn't need to know anything else. Dhonielle, however, seemed convinced it was going to hurt or that she was going to do it wrong. She had so many concerns that even Riley was starting to feel anxious about the change.

Then they turned off the main road onto the dusty private road that led to Wax & Wayne. As the van joined a line of other cars bouncing into the woods, the wolf cuff Riley had selected at Auntie Fang's forge when she was nine shivered against her wrist. The braided band of silver did this every time she crossed the wards of Wax & Wayne, but tonight it meant that she was one step closer to becoming a wolf. A tiny shudder of excitement danced down her spine. Even Dhonielle stopped talking at that moment.

The rest of the drive was short but seemed to take forever. Nearly every werewolf in the three counties that made up the Wax & Wayne Alliance was making their way into camp and it seemed they were all in front of their van, clogging up the narrow road. There were wolves all over the world, of course, but they were very good at hiding in plain sight. It helped that most of the stories about werewolves were just a little bit wrong, even if there was a touch of truth to them.

Finally, they emerged into an already crowded parking lot with rows and rows of cars. The second they were out of the van, Uncle Will shouted, "You two stick together! I'll be right behind you."

On the far side of the parking lot, Marcus Wayne stood atop an old-fashioned horse and cart, shouting directions at all the young pups. Marcus was a broad-chested white man with arms covered in snaking tattoos. He owned Wax & Wayne with his partner, Anthony Wax, who preferred doing paperwork to anything else.

"Load it up, load it up, pups! Remember, if tonight is the night you transform, your parents will be collecting your things, so do them a favor and make sure you've tagged everything clearly with your name. There's a box of Sharpies right here," Marcus bellowed. "What happens to the untagged goods?"

"You get a new wardrobe!" the more experienced kids shouted gleefully.

Riley smiled at the familiar sight. She would miss things about camp: games of hide-and-call, magic challenges and scavenger hunts, the thrill of getting to experiment with more advanced forms of lithomancy. But she'd learned all she could, and now she was ready to put it into practice and become a full member of the pack.

"There's Stacey," Dhonielle said quietly, pointing toward a girl with bright pink glasses who was waving in their direction.

Riley took off at a run. Stacey Strickland had been Riley's best friend since second grade when they'd been the only two werewolves in their class. It was hard having a secret like being a werewolf. Especially as they got older. While other kids wondered about pimples and starting periods at awkward moments, werewolf kids lived their whole lives knowing one day they'd sprout hair over every inch of their bodies and howl at the moon. It made puberty seem a little less impressive.

"Eeeee!" Stacey was saying. Stacey had a round face that matched her round body, and her hot-pink glasses had diamonds in the corners. She had skin that tanned easily and short brown hair, and she was always the last one to fall asleep at sleepovers. Right now, her eyes were so wide, they looked like they might never close again.

"Riley! It's finally tonight!" Stacey shrieked. "Hey, Dhonielle. You're gonna be a wolf! Oh, teeth and claws, I'm so excited, I could pee. Right here. Right now."

"Please don't." Riley took one step away, but Stacey laughed and linked her arm through Riley's and whispered, "I'm just so happy for you. There are *so* many things I can't wait to talk about. Wolf things. And as soon as I'm done with camp and you've returned to biped status, we are having a major sleepover. Deal?"

"Deal," Riley agreed as happiness bubbled up inside her.

"Strickland!" a voice called. It took Riley a minute to recognize the voice of Willow Oswald, the alpha of Stacey's prime.

"Eep! Gotta go, but I'll be there tonight cheering you on, okay?"

She pulled Riley into a quick hug before darting off in the direction of the campers. Riley watched the rest of Stacey's prime fold around her, sweeping her away before Riley could even say goodbye. It left an uncomfortable feeling in Riley's chest that she didn't like.

"Hey." Dhonielle tapped her on the shoulder. "You ready?"

Riley mustered a smile and nodded. "Yep."

The two of them followed the line of parents and children out of the parking lot, through the sharp clutch of honey locust trees guarding the far edge of the woods, and over the wooden bridge spanning Blood Creek.

Riley had walked this trail a hundred times. She knew it backward and forward. She knew where the roots bowed out of the ground from years of runoff, where it turned steep, and where it ran parallel to the creek. But tonight, the entire trail glittered with wolflight dust. Tiny particles of stone illuminated with lithomancy. The light beneath their feet would shine for hours yet, long enough for parents to return to the parking lot after the ceremony.

Riley kicked her foot through the dust, laughing as it drifted down like a shimmering rain. Dhonielle followed suit with a tentative kick, and the two of them raced through the dust until their hair and skin and shoulders glittered.

They emerged from the wooded path at the edge of camp just as the sun was making its final dive toward the horizon. The familiar ring of cabins spread out before them, each one lit up and ready to receive campers a little later tonight.

The air already smelled like smoke and the buzzing of excited chatter drew them toward the amphitheater. Here, the land dipped gradually down, curving in a wide bowl to make space for rows of wooden benches arranged around a massive bonfire.

Before Riley's first Full Moon Rite, Darcy had warned

her not to sit too close to the fire, saying, "It's June. In Kansas. No one needs a fire." And it was true. Even seated in the middle of the amphitheater that first time, Riley could feel the heat licking at her cheeks and forehead. She and her friends had moved farther back in the rows every year after that. This year, she wouldn't have a choice of where to sit.

"I spy with my little eye . . . two twelve-year-olds!" a familiar voice called as they approached the end of the path.

Tris Kelly was short and broad across the belly with a puff of blond hair that always bore a streak of rainbow flare. Today, a single stripe of electric blue arched over the crown of their head from just above their left temple. Riley knew the color was a result of transformational magic and that it had taken a lot of skill to achieve. Tris was one of those lucky wolves who transformed when they were nine and had been experimenting with magic ever since. Now, they were head counselor, and they were everyone's favorite.

Once upon a time, Riley had thought she might also like to be head counselor, but now that she was done with Tenderfoot Camp, she couldn't imagine going back.

"Anderson and Callahan," Tris called, "I've got special seats for you."

Riley did her best to control her smile as Tris led them around the back of the amphitheater to the section where the twelve-year-old tenderfoot contingent sat together. Since this was their final Full Moon Rite, it was easier to put them together. There were only nineteen this year, and almost everyone was there already. Riley knew them all by name, but her eyes landed on one: Lydia Edgerton.

Lydia sat in the middle of the group as though she were the natural sun of this little solar system. Her blond hair was loosely curled around her rosy cheeks, and it shone like pale gold in the firelight. She was tall and effortless compared to Riley, with creamy white skin. It didn't matter what she said; people always listened to her. Like now. She spoke, gesturing at the sky with an easy smile, and everyone around her laughed.

"Hey, Riley," she said, her big brown eyes sparkling. "Full Moon or First Wolf?"

"What?" Riley asked, feeling like she was wading into a trap, but Lydia merely repeated the question, "Full Moon or First Wolf?"

"Um, First Wolf, I guess?"

"Dhonielle?" Lydia tipped her head toward Dhonielle.

"Same, please," Dhonielle answered in a small voice.

"First Wolf it is," Lydia announced magnanimously, reaching into one of two paper bags Riley hadn't noticed before. But she frowned when her hand reached the bottom of the bag. "Oh, sorry. I've only got Full Moons left. Hope that's okay."

"She made them!" Aracely Bravo announced cheerfully, black curls twisting around her light brown shoulders. She was always cheerful. At least, Riley couldn't remember a time when she wasn't smiling or humming or gleefully telling someone way too many details about dinosaurs. "Isn't that amazing? I can't even make toast. The best part is that First Wolf howls when you put it in your mouth, and Full Moon glows!"

"I was at the Sweet Tooth yesterday and the uncles just got all of this equipment for making candy, and I thought we all deserved a treat for making it to our twelfth summer." Lydia shrugged as though it were no big deal that she'd whipped up a batch of homemade magic candy for everyone.

"Is it alchemy?" This question came from Kenver Derry. They were slender and always exceedingly well dressed, but other than that, all Riley knew about them was that they were really good at magic. They held an unwrapped piece of Lydia's candy in their palm to inspect it.

"It is!" Lydia turned to Kenver. "Sugar has so much potential energy in it, and once you add the water, you can almost treat it like lithomancy."

"I don't think I would have thought of that." Kenver's voice suggested they were deeply impressed.

A tight feeling settled in Riley's chest, and she pinched her lips together to prevent them from pouting. She was also impressed. She'd spent all day trying to magic a grape into a rock, and Lydia had created something special and unique that she could share with everyone.

Annoyed with herself and Lydia and magic all at once, Riley responded before she could stop herself. "Candy's not really my thing," she said, tossing her piece back to Lydia.

"Oh." Lydia looked disappointed. "I'm sorry. I would have brought you something else if I'd known."

It was just a piece of candy. But it didn't feel that way to Riley.

"Let's sit over here." Dhonielle tugged Riley toward empty seats near the end of a row, right next to Luke Shacklett.

Luke had shoulders that promised to be broad and sandy blond hair that he kept neatly trimmed. His skin was always lightly tanned and his fingernails crusted with dirt. Like Lydia, Luke was good at being in charge. All he had to do was smile or laugh or look at a person and they would agree with anything he said.

Just like Mama C.

Just like Riley wanted to be.

"I think you might have hurt her feelings," Luke said as Riley carefully sat so that her leg was not touching his.

"It's just a piece of candy," she answered quickly, noting the way Luke raised a suspicious eyebrow at her.

"Riley! Hey! Riley!" Milo's voice fired from her right.

He'd found a seat across the aisle and had caught her attention for the sole purpose of making kissy faces.

"Is your brother pretending to be a fish?" Luke asked.

"Yeah. The kind that suck slime off the aquarium," Riley said, refusing to let Milo embarrass her with something as mundane as kissy faces.

"Like a suckerfish?"

Riley was momentarily surprised that Luke knew its name, but she nodded. "Yeah, he definitely sucks."

Luke laughed, and then Riley did, too. It made her forget all about Lydia and her magic candy. It didn't matter anyway. All that mattered was becoming a real wolf.

A few more stragglers filed into the amphitheater and the crowd hushed as a woman with sandy-brown hair, pale white skin, and very pink lips made her way down the aisle. Riley knew her as well as any tenderfoot pup. Bethany Brooks, also known as Bethany Books, was the Keeper of the Roots and Rites, which was a fancy way of saying she was responsible for knowing and leading the major wolf rituals. Firelight glanced off her light blue glasses and illuminated the overlarge tome clutched in her hands as she approached the bonfire.

Bethany stopped in front of the flames and turned to face the crowd. Her gaze brought everyone to silence. The moon appeared above the trees, full and bright against the dark sky. The only sound was the crackling fire.

Riley felt a small electric shift in the air around her.

The Full Moon Rite was starting.

4

THE FULL MOON RITE

After a torturously long pause, Bethany opened the book and began to read in her strong, steady voice.

"Many moons ago, wolf magic was wild and dangerous, and as a result, wolves were hunted nearly to extinction. But that all changed with one wolf, First Wolf, whose name has been lost though her magic remains. She had no pack, no family, no protections from the great hunters and witches who crave wolf blood and wolf magic. Most of her life she spent running, unable to control her own transformations, unable to ensure those like her would not suffer from the same wild magic that lashed young wolves to the full moon."

Riley twisted in her seat to look for her moms. She found Mama N standing at the very edge of the amphitheater with Uncle Will amid all the proud, anxious faces. As promised, Stacey was among the pups returning to Tenderfoot Camp this year. She bounced and waved when she spotted Riley. But there was no sign of Mama C yet.

Riley returned her attention to Bethany. She'd heard this all many times before and knew the story of First Wolf by heart. Before her, werewolves had been forced to transform under the full moon—every full moon—and the magic made them ferocious and feral. It was a terrible way to live, which is why most wolves used to die young. But after coming to the New World in search of freedom and finding very little, First Wolf had had enough. She cast a powerful spell with her last call that ensured all the wolves who came after her would only transform for their first time on the full moon. After that, they would be able to choose.

"It's gonna happen," Dhonielle whispered. "Okay, okay, okay. It's gonna be okay."

Riley took her cousin's hand in hers and squeezed. "It's gonna be better than okay," she promised.

Riley dared a glance at Luke and then Lydia. There was no doubt in her mind that the two of them would become the alphas of their primes. They were both so calm and assured. Just like Mama C. They held authority without even trying.

There was no controlling who became pack leader and no predicting it either. Not even being the child of Cecelia Callahan was enough to ensure Riley would become an alpha. Darcy hadn't. But Darcy was more like

Mama N. She was thoughtful and strong and happiest when she wasn't in charge. But when Riley looked at Mama C, she wanted nothing more than to be just as capable and kind, just as trustworthy and smart.

She knew she could be. She only needed the opportunity to prove it.

A howl pierced the night sky. It was echoed on all sides of the amphitheater. Above them, the sky shimmered pink to green to dark blue. Riley recognized this from previous years. It was a sound shield, a secret keeper, and it would keep all the non-werewolves of Lawrence from hearing an entire pack of wolves howling just outside of the city.

Riley twisted the wolf cuff on her wrist. Every tenderfoot in the amphitheater wore something similar—bands of silver woven or hammered or twisted in unique designs. For the past three years, Riley's cuff had allowed her to pass through the wards of Wax & Wayne, but tonight, finally, it would also protect her from being spotted in wolf form.

Two figures strode down the aisles and stood before the bonfire.

First was Great Mathilda Williams, an older woman with short silver hair, eyes like daggers, and weathered brown skin. Next was Great Ansel Mort, who was younger than Mathilda by a few decades but still old. He was both tall and stout, with arms and legs that were sturdy as tree trunks. They were two of the three great pack leaders of the Wax & Wayne Alliance. Next to them should have been Great Cecelia Callahan. But Mama C wasn't here.

Riley sat up in alarm, nearly crying out. She heard Milo's quiet "Lilee?" from across the aisle and twisted in her seat to find Mama N. She and Uncle Will were deep in conversation with someone Riley couldn't see, their backs turned to the crowd. Then a face appeared in the gap between their shoulders. Black hair, tanned skin, and a nose like a beak. Riley recognized him right away as Crow, one of Mama C and Aunt Alexis's prime. And he didn't look happy.

They continued to speak with their heads tipped together. Then, suddenly, Mama N turned and caught Riley's eyes.

Instantly, Riley knew that something was wrong.

Mama N raised a hand as if to stop Riley from lunging out of her seat, which is exactly what Riley wanted to do. She mouthed, *Stay there,* and then she and Uncle Will hurried after Crow.

Little spikes of panic settled in Riley's lungs. It had to be Mama C. Something had to have happened to her, and Riley was desperate to know what, but Dhonielle squeezed her hand and said, "This is it!"

Great Williams's strong voice snapped in the air:

"Young wolves! Listen! When you hear the last call of First Wolf, join our run!"

It was time.

Before their eyes, the transformation rippled through the great pack leaders. They tucked their chins and rolled their shoulders forward, bending as gracefully as stems of wheat in the breeze. Their bodies shimmered as the transformation began, shivering down the length of their bodies. Soon their noses were long, their teeth sharp, their ears tall. Soon their bodies were covered in coats of fur and paws pressed against the earth instead of hands and feet. Soon two wolves stood where the great pack leaders had been, their outlines dark against the burning fire.

They raised their heads and released a single crooning note. Around the amphitheater, more followed, filling the air with a haunting cry that made Riley's breath catch in her throat. It was the most beautiful sound. She longed to add her voice to that chorus and in just a few moments, she *would*.

The song came to an abrupt end. Then the two wolves raced up the aisles, past the waiting rows of parents and siblings, and into the dark woods.

Silence fell again as each and every tenderfoot pup waited to see if they would hear the call. Riley held her breath until her heart pounded loudly in her ears. She would hear it. She would hear it any second.

"Wow. Do you hear that?" a voice whispered.

Riley listened and listened, but there was nothing. That was when she noticed the way several others had lifted their heads, the way their eyes were unfocused, their bodies tensed. It was a look she recognized. It was a look she'd seen on dozens of other children over the years as she awaited her turn.

Something heavy formed in Riley's stomach as she realized what was happening: they were hearing the call.

And she was not.

One by one, children stood up and moved toward the aisles. Riley watched them with a growing sense of discomfort. Next to her, Luke stood up, head tilted toward the call Riley still could not hear.

She closed her eyes. Took a deep breath. And listened.

She heard the crackle of the fire, the hurried pounding of feet up the aisle as tenderfoot pups began to leave, the occasional inhale or exhale from Dhonielle. But nothing else.

"I don't hear anything," Riley said out loud this time. Her voice sounded funny in her ears. Pinched, flattened, tight.

Riley opened her eyes.

"Riley?"

Riley spun in her seat to find her little brother was standing. His green eyes were as wide as moons and his shoulders were climbing toward his ears.

"Milo? Are you okay?" Riley asked, reaching for her little brother.

Milo nodded. Then shook his head. Then nodded again. "I hear it."

Riley stilled. "What?"

Now Milo's eyes cut away from hers. He looked at the ground, at the fire, at the sky, at anything except his sister.

"But—" Riley swallowed. "But you're only nine!"

Milo avoided her gaze.

"But it's *my* year," she said softly. It wasn't his fault. She knew that, and yet, this was her last chance. Part of her felt like he was taking something that belonged to her even though she knew it didn't work that way.

"Riley." Dhonielle tugged gently on her shoulder. "He has to go."

Anger crashed through Riley's chest, making her breath come in quick, ragged bursts. All around her, children were running toward the woods. They were laughing and howling and shouting goodbye to their parents. All the things Riley should be doing in this moment.

Milo took a small step back, head tilting again toward the call Riley could not hear. He tried lifting his eyes, but they got stuck somewhere around her shoulder.

"I'm sorry, Riley," he said sadly, and then he turned to hurry after the others.

Riley closed her eyes. She didn't want to see them go.

She wanted this to be a mistake. It had to be a mistake. It had to, so she listened.

And listened.

And listened.

In a way, it all started with First Wolf. People forget, or maybe they don't want to admit, that she made a deal with a witch. It is not true that witches and wolves are natural enemies, you know. Once we were great friends.

But here is the part of the story that doesn't get told: First Wolf was in love with a witch. More importantly, the witch was in love with First Wolf. When First Wolf asked her for help in freeing all wolves from the rhythms of the moon, the witch could not refuse.

They found the spell in the oldest book of shadows, The Book of Whispers, and like all great spells, it required a great sacrifice.

In order to ensure that every wolf after her would be able to choose when to transform, First Wolf had to give up her own magic. Or, rather, she pushed it into a call that would echo through generations of wolves on the night of the first full moon of summer.

That same spell made our magic one that must maintain balance. If one wolf possesses too much, others must possess less. If one steals the wolves of others, then some must have nothing to steal. There is no way to avoid this. The magic will choose.

And I'm afraid, dear ones, that if you are reading this, it has chosen you.

5

WOLFLESS

Riley couldn't hear anything.

No matter how quiet she tried to be, nothing called to her. It was several minutes before she realized that everything had become quiet around her and silence blanketed the amphitheater like a heavy snow. She opened her eyes and immediately wished that she hadn't.

Everyone was looking at her.

Every remaining tenderfoot pup and every single parent still in the back rows, they all stared. The only sound was that of the fire cackling as though darkly amused while everyone else held their breath in horror.

This simply didn't happen. Every single tenderfoot pup changed by the time they turned twelve. No exceptions. None.

Tears burned in Riley's eyes, but she blinked furiously against them. She would not cry. She would not cry. She would not cry in front of all these people.

A sob broke the silence. It took Riley a minute to re-alize it wasn't coming from her.

Swiveling in her seat, she was surprised to discover she wasn't alone.

Dhonielle was still seated next to her. She'd caved in on herself, her knees pulled up against her chest. She'd made herself so small, Riley hadn't even noticed that she was still here.

Then there was Kenver Derry. They were staring down at their hands, twisting their wolf cuff around, then pinching up little bits of dirt and transforming them into flower petals and crushing them to pulp.

Aracely Bravo was the source of the sobs. She had her face pressed into her hands and her wild, curly hair shuddered with every cry. Standing farthest from them was Lydia Edgerton. Her cheeks burned bright red, and she avoided looking directly at anyone.

Riley clenched her teeth. She wasn't alone. And some-how that made everything feel worse.

"Wolfless."

The whisper hissed from the crowd, amplified so that it landed crisply in Riley's ears. She felt it like an electric shock.

Wolfless was a word only suited for nightmares. It was a threat, a curse, and an insult. It was a fate no one ever dreamed was real.

Riley remembered the first time she'd heard that

word. It was years ago at Stacey's ninth birthday party and sleepover. After her parents had gone to bed, they'd all stayed awake telling spooky stories to one another. Heidi Marr told one about the Nameless Witch who tricks wolves into giving her their names so she might control their magic; Paislee Scott told one about the Hunter of Quickly Green who captured and killed countless wolves. Dhonielle had surprised them all by telling a story about the Devouring Wolf, who had the power to make someone wolfless—the same Devouring Wolf Riley had used to torment Milo at dinner tonight.

They'd shrieked with delight at the story because none of it was true. Some people chose not to transform, and obviously people like Mama N could be turned into Moon Bite wolves, but nothing could actually make a person wolfless.

Right?

"We're wolfless!" Aracely wailed.

"That's not possible," Riley said, but her lips felt numb.

A murmur started to swell around them. Riley searched the crowd for any sign of her moms, then her gaze fell on Stacey. Riley's best friend stared back at her with her mouth stuck in a small O of surprise.

In spite of the fire and the summertime warmth, Riley suddenly felt very, very cold.

"What's happening?" Dhonielle whispered helplessly. "I'm scared. I don't understand."

Riley didn't understand either. All she knew was that she didn't want to be here anymore.

As the murmuring grew louder, something shifted, bursting the bubble that seemed to hold everyone in stasis. Parents pressed forward, heading straight for them, while Tris cried from the back, "Tenderfoot pups with me! Move it!"

The tenderfoot pups trotted after Tris, whispering hurriedly to one another. The rest of the adults left more slowly and seemed less concerned with staring openly at the small group of untransformed twelve-year-olds. Riley scowled back at them. Then, suddenly, the parents were there, scooping up Lydia and Aracely and Kenver in their arms.

Riley searched once more, but her moms weren't here. Neither were Aunt Alexis and Uncle Will.

She and Dhonielle were alone.

"Riley." Her cousin's voice was almost too small to hear. "Riley, what's happening? Do you know what's happening?"

"No," Riley answered.

"But do you think something is wrong? With us?"

"There's nothing wrong with me," Riley snapped. Anger was bubbling up in her throat, and every time she opened her mouth, a little bit escaped.

"Okay, but—"

"Wolfless!" Aracely said again, tears streaming down her warm brown cheeks. "We're cursed!"

"Hush, baby." Aracely's mom smoothed the tears from her face as she spoke, her words softened by her accent.

Mr. Wayne was coming down the aisle now, chewing up the path with his long, powerful stride while Bethany floated along behind him. Mr. Wayne wasn't one of the three great pack leaders, but as the steward of Wax & Wayne, he held almost as much authority. This was neutral territory and Mr. Wayne's rule was as good as law. He looked as angry as Riley felt, and that was the first thing that made her feel a little bit better.

He held up his hands and shook his head as all of the parents started speaking at once.

"I don't know anything more than you do," he said.

The parents erupted again, peppering Mr. Wayne with questions he clearly could not answer. Bethany Books swept her arms out toward Riley and the others and gestured for them to leave the parents alone, like a mother duck shooing her ducklings away from danger.

The five of them shuffled nearer the fire, which Riley didn't mind so much right now. The warmth felt good on her cold skin.

"I know this is all confusing, but just sit tight and try not to worry," Bethany soothed. She pulled a little packet of tissues from her skirt pocket and offered it to Aracely, then returned to join the adults' conversation.

"How are we supposed to *not* worry about this?" Aracely punctuated her question with a hiccup that made her curls bounce.

"I wish they would talk a little louder. I can't hear any-thing they're saying," Lydia murmured, eyeing her uncles. Lydia's parents had died in a car accident when she was just a baby and her uncles had raised her ever since.

"They're probably just as confused as we are," Kenver suggested. They sat down on the bench and continued turning dirt into flower petals, then crushing them angrily.

"Why are you doing that?" Aracely asked.

Kenver shrugged. "Magic problems usually have magic solutions, right? I thought maybe I didn't transform be-cause my magic was blocked, but . . ." They let another demolished petal fall. "It still works."

"I knew something like this was going to happen." Dhonielle's voice quivered. "I just knew it. All day, I had such a bad feeling. Did anyone else? Did you feel like something bad was about to happen? And now this."

Riley recalled the growl. The hot breath on her neck. The gravelly voice that whispered, *Little wolf, little wolf, here I come.* She repressed a shiver.

Dhonielle was still talking. She only ever talked this much when she was scared. It was why she was impossible to play games like hide-and-call with. "But what did we do? Did we do something wrong? Or is there just something wrong with us? Maybe we're sick. Maybe we caught something that's delaying our transformation. A virus or something."

"We're not sick," Riley said, watching the adults closely. They were huddled together, Mr. Wayne a head taller than the others. He was speaking, but she couldn't hear a word.

"Maybe we're not really twelve!" Aracely paused to blow her nose. It honked like a goose.

"All five of us?" Lydia asked gently. "Seems unlikely that all five of our birthdays could be a year off, don't you think?"

"It could happen," Aracely said, but she didn't sound like she really believed it.

"Do you think it has something to do with our moms?" Dhonielle asked, her fear spinning off in yet another direction. "With where they are? Something bad must have happened for them not to be here, right? Do you think they're okay?"

Riley was worried about the same thing, but she didn't want to say it. Mama C always said that part of being a leader was keeping it together when things got tough. Not panicking at the drop of a hat.

Dhonielle kept going. "Maybe something really big has happened. Maybe this is just one symptom of a larger

56

problem. Or maybe wolf magic is dying?! It could have to do with climate change or something. Magic is connected to the earth like everything else. What if we're killing the magic the same way we're killing the planet?!"

"But . . ." Aracely's bottom lip trembled. "But that's not our fault. I recycle!"

Dhonielle opened her mouth to speak again. This time, Riley got there first.

"Dhonielle! You're not helping!"

Dhonielle stopped. Her mouth clamped shut and big tears welled in her eyes.

Lydia stepped between the two of them, wrapping an arm around Dhonielle's narrow shoulders. "It's going to be okay," she said.

Riley's heart was pounding. She shouldn't have gotten upset with Dhonielle, but she'd had to do something. And here Lydia was doing something better. Soothing Dhonielle when Riley had let anger get in the way. She wasn't behaving very much like a leader after all.

She barely noticed that the adults had stopped their private conference and were coming toward them. Their expressions ranged from frustrated to the kind of concern Riley associated with true danger.

"Pups," Mr. Wayne began in a grave tone, his thick eyebrows furrowed together. "We don't know what's happening to you, that's the truth."

"But we're not, I mean, we aren't—" Kenver's voice

faded to a whisper before adding the final word: "Wolf-less?"

"We don't think so. But we need some time to figure things out. Which means"—he pursed his lips as though he'd tasted something sour—"unfortunately, the only thing we can do tonight is gather information. So we're going to send you all home while we do that and circle up in the morning. Okay? Just try to get some rest tonight."

While the others turned to their parents and started to head home, Mr. Wayne cleared his throat and smiled uncomfortably at Riley and Dhonielle. "Pups, I need to tell you something."

"Is this about our parents?" Riley asked, trying to ignore the way her chest tightened at Mr. Wayne's nod.

"They're okay, but Dhonielle, your mom got caught in a hunter's snare while they were in the South Wood. Now, just remember that I've already said they're okay."

Dhonielle pressed her lips together, doing her best not to cry.

"A hunter got through the wards?" Riley asked, forgetting everything else.

For as long as there had been werewolves, there had been werewolf hunters. All the way back before the time of First Wolf. But Wax & Wayne, all 1,200 acres of Kansas wilderness, was supposed to be protected and fortified. The wolves had owned it since the early 1800s when the first five families arrived, and they'd done everything they could to ensure its safety, including setting up wards that alerted the pack when someone crossed them.

Riley couldn't remember ever hearing about werewolf hunters getting this close before. If hunters were here now, then they were all in danger. No wonder Mama C hadn't returned in time for the Full Moon Rite.

"As far as we can tell, that's what happened. Crow came back to let us know, and Nina and Will have gone to help bring them in," he said, referring to Mama N and Uncle Will. "It shouldn't be long now."

"Okay," Dhonielle said, her eyes darting nervously to her cousin.

Riley swallowed hard. There were plenty of reasons for Dhonielle to be afraid, but Rule #2 in Cecelia Callahan's Alpha Code was very clear: *Encourage others.* Riley put a hand on Dhonielle's arm and gave it a squeeze.

"We'll wait together," Riley said, and in spite of everything, seeing the relief on Dhonielle's face made her feel a little better, too.

They say that perhaps he could have recovered if the losses had not been so severe, but after his family died, his magic withered inside him. He could no longer transform with the pack, no longer run through the woods or lift his voice with ours.

He became wolfless. And there was nothing anyone could do to help him.

That was when he sought out the witch.

6

HOME . . . AGAIN

An hour later, Mama C was back. So was Aunt Alexis. The two sisters swept into the amphitheater with Mama N and Uncle Will hard on their heels. Neither one of them looked good, but Aunt Alexis looked like she'd been dragged through the underbrush for an hour, with scrapes and dried mud splashed across her pale cheeks and dark circles beneath her eyes.

She was clearly wounded and exhausted, but she didn't let that stop her. The second she spotted Dhonielle, she had her in her arms.

Mama C approached more slowly. Her dark brown hair frayed out of its ponytail, her eyes were tight with exhaustion, but she was still Great Callahan, and just seeing her made Riley feel a little bit safer.

Instead of wrapping Riley in a smothering hug as the other parents had done, Mama C placed her hands on Riley's shoulders and looked into her eyes.

"I'm here now," she said. "Everything will be okay."

Riley believed her. Or Riley *wanted* to believe her, so she nodded and swallowed the tears that threatened to explode from her face like a summer storm.

They all left together and the whole ride home was quiet. Riley was glad to be alone in the back seat, where no one could try to make her smile or talk or do anything except concentrate on resisting the urge to cry. But for some reason, it was only getting harder the closer they got to home.

The instant Mama N put the car in park, Riley was unbuckled and pounding her way up the porch steps to the front door, where she suddenly remembered that she could not open it because her keys were inside, hanging on a hook on the old hall tree.

She stared at the knob, its brassy finish patchy and dull after years of use. She wasn't supposed to have to unlock this door for a month. She wasn't supposed to be here. She was supposed to be in the woods. She was supposed to be a wolf with a prime pack and no use for keys or doorknobs or porches. Riley's cheeks began to burn, her palms began to sweat. How had everything gone so, so wrong?

Her frustration boiled up inside her until she kicked the door. She knew it was childish and she shouldn't have done it, but it did make her feel a little better.

Her moms didn't join her right away. She could hear them whispering behind her on the driveway. She couldn't hear what they said, but she could imagine.

They were talking about her. They were probably just as horrified to have a child who hadn't transformed as she was to be one. They were probably wondering what was wrong with her.

Finally Mama N reached over Riley's shoulder and calmly turned the key in the lock. Riley barged into the house and headed for the stairs.

"Riley," Mama N said before she'd taken three steps.

Mama N dropped her purse on the hall tree as Mama C flipped the light switch. They all three flinched, blinking as their eyes adjusted to the light in the big, empty house.

"I don't want to talk about it," Riley answered, her voice quivering. "I just want to go to bed."

"Going to sleep won't make this go away." This was one of Mama N's favorite sayings, but it wasn't usually attached to something as monumentally terrible as this. "Talking about it will help."

"How?"

Riley looked between her moms. Her question sounded sullen and stubborn, but it was also real. If talking was somehow going to help her become a wolf, then she wanted to know.

Mama N sighed lightly in that way she did when she thought Riley had intentionally misinterpreted her words.

"Because sometimes when we're angry or upset, it helps to figure out why."

"But I know why." Everyone knew why. That was part of the problem, and she didn't understand why Mama N wanted to pretend that talking would to fix anything.

"The important thing right now is not to panic." Mama N turned to Mama C, and Riley knew they were about to gang up on her with Rule #1. Parents always did that.

"That's right," Mama C said in her deep, calm voice. "Panic will only get in the way. Bethany is going to do some research tonight and we'll know more in the morning. Information is our friend here."

"This wouldn't have even happened if you'd been at the Full Moon Rite instead of off in the South Wood!" Riley knew it wasn't rational, but she was angry and part of her did wonder if things would have been just fine if Mama C had been at the rite.

Mama C pressed her lips into a flat line and didn't respond.

"Riley, that's not fair," Mama N said. "Sometimes things don't go how we expect them to, and that doesn't mean you've done anything wrong or that there's anything wrong with you. It just means things are going to work out differently for you."

"Differently?" Riley couldn't believe her ears. "Things don't work out differently for wolves! They work the same way! We hear the call, we transform. There's no other way!"

"Riley, please don't shout." Mama C crossed her arms

over her chest and trained a disapproving look on Riley.

"You may not have turned tonight, but there's more than one way to become a wolf," said Mama N.

This part was true. There were two ways: to be born a wolf, or to choose to become one. Someone who chose to become a werewolf would receive a bite on the night of the full moon and their first transformation would follow. It was how families brought in the people they loved. It was how Mama N had become a wolf.

But there was one major difference between a Moon Bite and a born werewolf: Moon Bites never formed a prime pack. Sure, they joined the larger pack, and in every other way they were full members of society. But they didn't get those four other wolves who were theirs. The four who would trust and support you for the rest of your life. It was a kind of magic that couldn't be replicated. And Riley wanted it.

"But I want to be a *real* wolf!" Riley shouted.

"Riley." Mama C's voice was sharp.

Mama N's lips tightened and she blinked rapidly. The hurt was plain on her face for a split second and then it was gone. Riley felt a new kind of twist in her stomach.

"I mean—" Riley slowly backed away, afraid of what she might say next. "You don't understand."

Mama N swallowed hard and nodded. "Maybe I don't. But this isn't the end of the world. I want you to remember that, okay? Wolf magic is about love and choice.

No matter what happens, you have options."

"Options?" Riley was almost shouting as she turned toward the stairs once more. "You don't know anything!"

"Riley," Mama N called, her voice a little more demanding now.

Riley stopped. She felt horrible all the way through. Like an apple with a rotten spot in the middle. She was so angry. Messy and volatile and confused. She wasn't sure she'd ever felt this angry before. With herself, with her moms, with the magic that had rejected her. And she knew she shouldn't be, but the feeling simply wouldn't stop.

"I love you," Mama N said.

Riley bit her bottom lip to keep from crying. She was supposed to say it back. That was how fights ended in the Callahan house. But she just couldn't.

"Whatever," she said, before darting up the stairs and down the hallway to her bedroom.

She flipped on the light and immediately regretted it. The room was precisely as she'd left it. The bed was made, the floor cleared and vacuumed, clothes hung neatly in her closet. Cottonwood and Oak were curled together at the foot of her bed, calico splotches on Cottonwood rolling seamlessly into Oak's brown tiger stripes. Nothing was out of place.

Except for her.

Riley rushed to her closet and ripped a dozen shirts

from their hangers, throwing them to the floor. Next, she went to her dresser, pulling open the middle drawer that contained all her summer shorts, folded and neatly stacked. She grabbed a handful and tossed them into the air. One landed on the cats, sending Cottonwood diving beneath the bed. Oak, however, merely peered at her through a dangerous slit in his cat eyes as if to say, *Mind the shorts, pup.*

Riley didn't stop there. She pulled books from her shelves, dumped out an entire box of colored pencils, and messed up her comforter. When she was done, her room looked normal and she felt calmer. But it was as if expending so much anger left space for something else to creep in, and suddenly Riley felt sad. It felt like a shadow with long arms that wrapped all the way around her shoulders.

Her lungs worked harder to draw a breath and her throat squeezed tight. Just as she fell face-first into her pillow, hot tears began to leak from her eyes.

Riley Callahan did not like to cry. Certainly not in public. Crying in private was only marginally better. It made her feel puffy and sluggish and, worse, like she'd done something wrong. Right now, it was all she wanted to do, so she pressed her face into the pillow and cried and cried and cried.

When she'd cried every tear her eyes could produce, she sat up and pushed open her window. The night air was thick with humidity and an owl sang far in the distance. The moon was high overhead and blisteringly bright.

Riley crouched on her knees, palms pressed to the windowsill, leaning forward so the breeze tickled the tip of her nose. She drew a deep breath. She smelled the grass Darcy had cut just yesterday, the sickly sweet grape-soda scent of Mama N's irises around the deck, and the vague fumes of paint thinner coming from the work shed. She was meant to be a wolf. She knew it the way she knew all of these scents.

Blowing out a breath, Riley closed her eyes and dropped her head down on her arms.

Crickets and frogs chirped all around, a dog barked once, leaves rustled in the big cottonwood nearby. Then the sounds of the night dropped away as though someone pressed mute on everything, and Riley heard a soft rumbling.

Riley's head snapped up and she gripped the windowsill. She held very still and listened again. The rumble returned. This time, it was closer, so close it was as if a wolf sat behind her, its muzzle hovering an inch from her head, teeth bared and gleaming in the moonlight.

A flock of shivers raced down Riley's backbone as she realized it was exactly like the growl she'd heard earlier that day.

For a moment, she was too terrified to move. Then a new feeling coursed through her like a surge of electricity. It felt like her body was on the brink of transformation, like maybe, just maybe, she was about to shift. She rose up on her knees and spotted the full moon through the window.

Just as Riley was daring to hope she was going to change, the sensation faded. All the familiar night sounds returned, and Riley was just a kid sitting alone on her bed.

7

IN WHICH THINGS
SEEM TO GET WORSE

Riley had a hard time sleeping after that. Every sound, whether it was the familiar creaking of the stairs or the faraway bark of a dog, made her snap to attention, afraid the growling had returned. By morning, she felt like her head was full of very heavy, very dense rocks.

She waited until she heard her moms up and moving around. Then she waited a little bit longer. She didn't want to face either of them, but it was unavoidable.

She peeled herself out of bed, dislodging Oak and Cottonwood from around her legs, then shuffled down the hall to the bathroom she shared with Darcy and Milo. Both of their toothbrushes stood on their chargers, their towels hung from hooks behind the door, and the rug next to the shower was still damp from Milo's last shower.

Right now, both of her siblings were wolves. Real wolves. Running with the pack out at Wax & Wayne.

And she was not.

It was an effort to reach out and take her own toothbrush. Every step of her morning routine felt heavier than usual, and she couldn't stop the refrain in her head that sang, *Not a wolf, not a wolf, not a* real *wolf.*

Slowly, she returned to her room and dressed for the day. She cobbled together an outfit from the tornado of clothing strewn across her floor, then made her way downstairs avoiding the squeaky steps. Maybe if she could get downstairs without her moms noticing, she could put off the inevitable conversation a little while longer.

"Riley," Mama C called from the kitchen.

Or they could be waiting to ambush her. Parent style.

Riley sighed, then took a deep breath and rounded the corner.

Cecelia Callahan was seated at the kitchen table with a cup of coffee in one hand and a tablet in the other. She'd showered recently and her wet hair was tied back in a low ponytail. It made her look more severe than usual. She was dressed in a simple brown T-shirt and jeans tucked down into her favorite pair of boots. Even plainly dressed, she looked commanding and wolfish in a way Riley was beginning to fear she herself never would.

"Nina is in the workshop," Mama C said. "Is there anything you would like to go say to her?"

Last night's argument rang loud and clear in Riley's

mind, and her stomach knotted tightly around the memory of Mama N's face when Riley had shouted that she wanted to be a real wolf. She knew she should apologize, but why didn't Mama N understand how much this meant to her? Didn't that matter?

Fresh anger warmed her cheeks. She shook her head and answered stubbornly, "No."

"Is there anything you'd like to say to me?"

What she wanted were answers. And Mama C had already proved that she had none of those. Again, Riley answered, "No."

"All right." Mama C nodded as if she'd been expecting Riley to be exactly as childish as she was being, and that made Riley feel worse. "Get some breakfast and then pack your camp bag."

"Wait. What? Why?" Riley's voice climbed high with panic.

"Because I've spoken with Ms. Broo—with Bethany, and we agree it will be best if the five of you kids are all in one place."

"But I can't go back to camp!" she shouted.

Mama C stood up calmly, as though Riley weren't having an emotional crisis in front of her. She took her coffee mug to the sink, dumped the dregs down the drain, then seemed to consider the countertop before setting it down slowly.

"Mom!" Riley cried. "You can't make me do this! I can't go to camp! All the tenderfoot pups there have either had their first transformation or they're not twelve yet. You can't make me go!"

"I don't listen to young ladies who raise their voices," Mama C said, brushing past Riley and all her concerns. "Pack up."

Riley felt her jaw drop. She didn't know that she'd ever been *young lady*'d before, certainly not by Mama C. But the thought of having to attend Tenderfoot Camp as a wolfless twelve-year-old was agonizing. Riley could already hear the whispers, could see the guarded looks, the fearful expressions. Worst of all would be the sympathy from Stacey. She had to find some way to stop this.

"But what if we're contagious?!" she called.

Mama C turned with eyebrows raised. "You mean, what if your condition can be transferred to other tenderfoot pups?"

"Yeah." Riley clung to her mom's attention now that she had it. "We don't know anything about what's happening, right? So what if it's like a virus or something? Shouldn't we stay away from camp? There are so many things we should be considering right now. That's Rule Number One, right?"

"Hmm?" Mama C asked as though she hadn't heard anything Riley had just said.

"Don't panic . . ." Riley started.

"Exactly," Mama C agreed without finishing the rule. "And right now, you're panicking for no good reason. You won't be attending Tenderfoot Camp, but we need all five of you at Clawroot while we sort things out."

"Clawroot?" Riley was momentarily stunned. Clawroot was the name of the small village tucked away in the midst of Wax & Wayne. It was where the pack met to discuss secret wolf matters, where they prepared big magic, and where some of them even lived. As the great pack leader, Cecelia Callahan spent a good deal of time there, but tenderfoot wolves rarely had any cause to go. Riley had only been twice.

"Better to have you together than spread out across town, right?"

"Oh," Riley answered as if the wind had been knocked from her lungs. "Yeah, I guess."

"I'm glad you're seeing sense. Now, get packed and meet me at the car."

"For how long?" Riley asked.

"We're not sure, so plan for at least a week."

Mama C left through the sliding glass door that opened into the backyard, leaving Riley alone. For a second, Riley considered sitting down and doing absolutely nothing. No one was listening to her. No one seemed to understand how devastating this was. But when it came down to it, the plan actually sounded okay. In fact, the more she thought of it, the better it sounded.

Here, she couldn't do anything except wait and wallow. At Clawroot, she would be able to help, and she'd be near the others, which was the first thing that brought a smile to Riley's face.

At least she wasn't alone.

8

AUNT ALEXIS

It was late in the day by the time Riley and Mama C made it to Clawroot. They hiked for a long while before they reached the outskirts of the village. The whole perimeter was surrounded by a ring of rock posts standing four feet high with a symbol shaped like a tree carved into each one. Beneath it were the words *Clawroot North Bead*.

Riley's wolf cuff shivered slightly as she passed between two of the posts marking the ward of Clawroot. Like the larger ward around all of Wax & Wayne, interior wards added extra layers of protection to various sites like Clawroot and Tenderfoot Camp. Crossing this one, Riley felt an echoing shiver in her spine.

They continued through the woods for a few more minutes before the trees fell away, leaving them at the top of a hill on the edge of a broad clearing in the center of which stood a village. Though Riley had been here before, the sight sent a thrill all the way down to her toes. For a second, all she could do was stare.

The Hall of Ancestors stood at the center of everything like a stately old wolf, its pale sandstone face traveling up into a sharply peaked roof as though howling at the sky. At least a dozen additional buildings were constellated around the hall, all stitched together by a series of flagstone pathways. The spaces between them were flooded with native wildflowers and tall grasses. The whole place felt like a magical village from a fairy tale.

Adjusting her camp duffel on her back, Riley followed Mama C down the hill where cottonwood fluff danced through the air like tiny feathers. They walked past the Hall of Ancestors, between two identical buildings from which wafted delicious, savory scents that teased Riley's stomach, to a row of smaller cabins perched at the edge of a stream.

Everywhere Riley looked she saw evidence of wolf magic, from the wolflights by each door to the wind chimes that howled softly in the breeze. But it was more than that. There were people and wolves wandering or hurrying between the cabins. A prime pack, just older than Darcy's, was practicing transformations in the field, trying to see which of them could shift fastest. Their bodies blurred between human and wolf so quickly, Riley could barely track the change.

It was hard to believe she was here to stay inside Clawroot. It should have been exciting, and for a second, it was. But then Riley remembered. She wasn't here

because she was a wolf. She was here because she wasn't.

A voice rang in her head. *Not a real wolf.*

"You five will be in this one." Mama C rested one hand on the railing of the cabin, giving Riley the opportunity to go first.

And suddenly, Riley was nervous. All the way here, she'd been so distracted by the thought of living at Clawroot that she hadn't stopped to think about all the people she'd be living *with.*

"We're staying together?" she asked. Apart from Dhonielle, she didn't really know the others very well, and now they were going to be sleeping side by side for who knew how long. The thought of sharing a bathroom with Lydia Edgerton made her feel very, very strange.

"Better to keep you all together," Mama C confirmed. "Besides, space out here is at a premium."

"Great Callahan!" a voice called.

Julie Montgomery, the caretaker of Clawroot, was racing across the field. She was a proud, fat woman with sparkling blue eyes and straight black hair that cut past pale pink cheeks to her chin, and she was fast.

"Great Callahan," Ms. Montgomery repeated as she skidded to a stop. "I'm afraid there's something—well, there's something you need to see." She glanced at Riley and added, "Hi, Riley. Mind if I borrow your mom for a bit?"

With Great Leaders Williams and Mort currently out

with the young wolves, Mama C was in charge of the entire Wax & Wayne Alliance. It was a great responsibility.

"Sure. I can go in on my own," Riley volunteered. It was always exciting to see her mom in action. The way the pack relied on her to provide steady guidance in the face of any problem. It made her feel proud to be the pup of Cecelia Callahan.

Mama C put a hand on Riley's shoulder and nodded. "I'll see you soon. Be good and mind Bethany."

"I will," Riley promised.

Ms. Montgomery led Mama C down the row of cabins to the one at the very end. Riley watched until she couldn't see them anymore. Then she climbed the three front steps and knocked twice.

"Come in!"

Riley pushed the door open and stepped inside. The cabin wasn't like the ones they'd used at Tenderfoot Camp, with their bunked beds and plastic mattresses. This was more like a home with a comfortable den carpeted by thick rugs and packed with overstuffed chairs.

"I'm back here." Kenver appeared in the doorway on the other side of the room, an old camera clutched in one hand. Their strawberry blond hair was bobbed around their ears and everything they wore from their shoes to their T-shirt was some shade of blue, including a swipe of shimmery blue lipstick that looked great against their peaches-and-cream skin.

The bedroom was a little bit bigger than the den, with three beds on one side and two on the other. Another door opened into a bathroom, and there were two windows on the back wall. Kenver's things were neatly piled in the center of the room.

"Hey, Kenver," Riley said, feeling awkward and trying not to show it. "Did you pick a bed?"

Kenver shook their head and crossed their arms over their chest. "No. What's the point?"

It seemed to Riley that the point was obvious—the beds near the windows were clearly superior to those by the bathroom—but she didn't get the impression that Kenver really wanted to talk about it. In any case, waiting did seem the most fair, so Riley dropped her own bag next to Kenver's and piled her sleeping bag on top.

Riley tried to think of something to say. A leader would set a good example. That was Rule #3 of Cecelia Callahan's Alpha Code: *A leader makes the pack.* Riley should set an example for Kenver. Then again, they weren't really a pack; they were just two pups suffering under the same circumstances.

"Hi," a quiet voice said from the door.

Riley spun to find Dhonielle had slipped inside the cabin and made it all the way to the bedroom without being heard.

"Hey, Riley. Kenver," she added, sounding like she might be afraid of her own voice.

Kenver offered a wave that somehow managed to be grumpy.

Riley thought that if she left the two of them alone, they might never speak again.

"We're putting our stuff there until everyone's here," Riley explained, gesturing to the bags. "Then we can pick beds so it's fair for everyone."

"If anything *can* be fair for us," Kenver muttered.

"That's a great idea, Riley," Dhonielle said, smiling a little as she added her things to the growing pile in the middle of the floor.

Kenver raised their old camera and aimed it at the pile. They shifted on their feet a little, studying the view-screen with a critical eye, then finally snapped the button.

"You got everything you need, little love?"

Aunt Alexis stepped inside the bedroom. She was a softer version of her older sister with the same dark brown hair and wintery-pale skin as Mama C. She was just a pinch taller, however, with long, willowy limbs and a gentle smile. In spite of that, she'd been formidable all Riley's life.

Now, though, there was something different about her. Her eyes had lost their warmth and she seemed to tower over them like a spindly old tree. Even her smile looked like it had been painted on as she surveyed the room.

"I'm good, Mom," Dhonielle said, hitching her shoulders a little.

"Are you okay, Aunt Alexis?" Riley asked.

Her aunt drew a deep breath and forced her smile a little wider. If she was trying to imitate a jack-o'-lantern, she was nailing it. "I'm fine. Don't worry about me. We need to worry about you five. Is your—" She paused, then started again. "Is CeCe here?"

Riley couldn't help but frown a little at that. Aunt Alexis and Mama C were in the same prime pack. Shouldn't she just *know* that she was nearby?

"Yeah, Ms. Montgomery took her to one of the other cabins to show her something," Riley answered.

Aunt Alexis nodded, then moved past Riley into the room. She ducked her head inside the bathroom to investigate, and when she was satisfied, she returned to Dhonielle.

"I want you"—she paused again and lifted her strange gaze to Riley and then Kenver—"all five of you to do exactly as you're told. Do not leave Clawroot for any reason, understand?"

"We understand," Riley and Dhonielle answered in unison.

"I guess," Kenver added with a roll of their eyes.

"Are there more traps out there? More hunters?" Riley asked, suddenly remembering that there was more than one mystery plaguing the wolves right now.

Aunt Alexis thought for a moment. "Perhaps."

All Riley knew about hunters' snares was that they were dangerous. Very, very dangerous. And she'd never really had to worry about them before. Then again, only wolves had to worry about hunters, and Riley wasn't one.

And suddenly Riley had an idea.

"Then maybe we can help!" Riley suggested, excited that their circumstances could prove useful in some way. "Since we . . ."

She stopped. She couldn't finish the sentence. It was still too surreal and admitting it out loud felt final in a way she wasn't prepared for. The voice in her head whispered, *Not a real wolf!*

"I mean, hunters' snares shouldn't hurt us, right?" she asked.

"You want to go to the South Wood to hunt for hunters?!" Dhonielle's voice was small and frightened.

"No." Aunt Alexis shook her head. "Remember what I just said? Do not leave Clawroot for any reason. We need you to sit tight while we figure things out. It's best if we just keep you together and safe."

Riley frowned but didn't protest. "Okay."

Aunt Alexis studied Riley for a moment as though she didn't believe Riley would follow instructions. Her gaze was harder than usual. Her hazel eyes looked flat and eerie, like a pond that offered no reflection. It was a relief when she looked away.

"Right. Come here and give me a hug, little love," she said, summoning her daughter into her arms.

She squeezed Dhonielle tight, pulled Riley in for a quick hug of her own, and then Aunt Alexis was gone.

9

THE BATTLE OF THE BEDS

"**W**hat did the snare do to her exactly?" Riley asked when she was sure Aunt Alexis was out of earshot.

Dhonielle shook her head and shrugged. "I didn't really get a chance to ask. As soon as we got home, she shifted and ran back out."

"She shifted?" Kenver asked, interest temporarily overwhelming their commitment to pouting. "That's odd."

"Why is it odd?" Riley asked.

"I've only heard some stories, but hunters' snares are what they use to expose a werewolf. If a wild wolf encounters one, they can run right through without getting hurt."

"I guess werewolf hunters aren't interested in regular wild wolves," Dhonielle murmured.

"Right, so they can run through a snare like it's nothing more than grass, but if a werewolf crosses one, they get trapped and forced out of their wolf." Kenver was speaking in a low, hurried voice. "Then the snare holds them there, just like a spider's web. The harder they struggle, the more the threads of magic stick to them. It's supposed to be very painful."

"But why is it odd that she shifted?" Dhonielle asked.

"Well, because from what I understand, after someone's been trapped in a hunters' snare, shifting is painful for a while, and they need to rest until they've recovered. Like when you burn your finger and you don't want to touch anything until it's better."

"Do you think it wasn't a snare?" Riley asked.

Kenver shrugged. "I'm just saying what I know."

"But why would they lie?" Dhonielle asked.

Riley didn't have an answer for that, but she was also thinking that it was even more odd that Aunt Alexis was caught in a snare on the same night they didn't transform.

"Helloooooo?" a voice called from the front door. "Anybody home? Ready or not, I'm coming in, and—oh, hi!"

Aracely trundled through the door carrying one, two, three, four bags in addition to her sleeping bag. Her face was glistening with sweat, but she was smiling, which was a change from last night when she'd been crying most of the time. She wore a T-shirt with a bright orange T-Rex on it that read SAVE THE DINOSAURS!

"Hi," Riley, Dhonielle, and Kenver said together.

"Have we chosen beds? Anybody care if I take this

one? I like the window," Aracely explained as she deposited her collection on one of the beds. "Oh, wow, this place is so cool. Way nicer than the summer camp cabins. There's not even plastic on this mattress!"

Aracely bounced a few times on the bed opposite the one she'd claimed with her stuff, then hopped up and headed into the bathroom before Riley could explain things.

"Oooh, a tub! That's fancy. At least we don't have to hike to a shower house or anything. I don't mind hiking, but my feet were always dirty by the time we got back. I mean, it's just dirt, but who wants to put dirty feet in the bottom of their sleeping bag?"

"Is she talking to us?" Dhonielle whispered.

Riley shook her head. "I really can't tell."

Aracely emerged from the bathroom. Half of her curls were tied in a little ponytail on top of her head while the rest bounced around her shoulders.

"What do you think they use this place for? Seems weird that there's an odd number of beds. Why not just four? Four is a good number for one toilet, if you know what I mean. Sharing a bathroom with five people is . . . a lot. And I'm speaking from experience here. Sisters stink just as much as brothers, for the record."

"They're for prime packs," Riley said, gesturing to the beds. "That's why there are five. Because primes stay here when they need to."

"That makes so much sense," Aracely said, nodding. "I guess it's lucky there's five of us, then."

"Lucky?" Riley asked.

"It kind of makes us a prime, if you think about it," Aracely answered.

Riley hadn't thought about it that way, and now that Aracely had pointed it out, she couldn't tell if it made her feel better because the five of them were in this together no matter what, or worse because they weren't a real prime.

"I don't know what that makes us," Riley said.

"Whatever we are, we're definitely a pack." Lydia's voice surprised them all.

Riley spun around. Lydia was standing in the doorway with a backpacking bag strapped to her shoulders and a sleeping bag clutched to her chest.

"Sisters-in-arms, right?" Aracely announced proudly.

Kenver flinched at that, mouth pinching tight. It reminded Riley of how uncomfortable Darcy used to be whenever anyone misgendered her. Now Darcy didn't hesitate to correct people, but it had taken practice.

"What? What did I say?" Aracely asked when no one answered her.

"We all know each other's names, but let's share pronouns," Riley suggested.

"But I know all the pronouns," Aracely answered

brightly. "We've only been going to camp together for-ever."

"But sometimes pronouns change," Riley answered. "I'm she/her."

Lydia, Dhonielle, and Aracely all repeated the answer, going around the circle clockwise.

When it was Kenver's turn, they cleared their throat and answered, "They/them."

"Oh!" Aracely cried. "I get it. Not sisters-in-arms, siblings-in-arms!"

Kenver almost smiled at that.

"Great. Now that that's settled, let's pick beds. Looks like Aracely already claimed that one. Do the three of you have a preference? I can sleep anywhere," Lydia said, easily stepping into the center of things and taking over like she always did.

"I like to be close to the bathroom," Kenver said.

"I'd like to be near a window," Dhonielle added.

"Riley?" Lydia asked.

In two seconds, Lydia had barreled through Riley's careful attempts to make a plan and lead by example. None of what Riley had done mattered; Lydia was in charge and everyone was listening to her.

"I—" Riley tried to find the response that would make her sound cool and collected. "I'll take whatever's left."

She felt pretty good about that until Lydia said, "How about you take the one over there, then? It looks newer than this one, and I don't mind a few lumps."

"That's so nice of you, Lydia," Dhonielle said admiringly.

Riley's cheeks warmed and she knew they were turning pink. Everyone was moving to their appointed beds while anger bubbled up in Riley's chest.

"Thanks," she said, even though she didn't feel very grateful.

Riley hauled her things over to her bed. Of course, she'd ended up on the side of the room with only two beds, and of course Lydia was in the other one. If Stacey were here, they'd have picked these two beds on purpose so they were close enough to whisper at night. It was hard to imagine whispering anything with Lydia.

As she unpacked, she tried to imagine how things should have gone. But no matter how many times she imagined herself divvying up the beds, Lydia always swooped in at the end and offered to take the lumpy bed. Like she was some kind of ghost of niceness. Haunting Riley with her good deeds.

"Now what?" Aracely asked, surrounded by a collection of stuffed animals that was truly impressive.

This time, Riley didn't give Lydia, Ghost of Nice Things, the chance to take the lead. She stood up and stepped into the center of the room. She may have lost the battle of the beds, but there were plenty more battles to win. "Let's go find out," she announced.

10

LIGHTS-OUT!

It turned out that dinner was next. In the time it had taken to sort the beds and unpack, afternoon had turned into evening and the residents of Clawroot were filing into the dining hall. The five of them had just left the cabin when Ms. Montgomery met them on the path.

"Oh, there you are. I'm sorry I was late, but I got caught up in . . . well, it doesn't matter," she said, clasping her hands together. "I think most of you know me, but I'm Julie Montgomery, she/her. I've come to show you around Clawroot and take you to dinner; does that sound good?"

Aracely nodded with an emphatic, "Mmhmm!"

"Actually, we wanted to know what we're supposed to do here," Riley said.

"Bethany is going to fill you in on that bit. Come and get some food and we'll find her." She spun around and started back down the stone path, talking over her shoulder as she went. "One tip about living in Clawroot:

Never be last for dinner. Once the young packs get in from patrolling, they'll scrape every pot and pan clean. You think I'm joking, but I've even seen them lick each other's plates clean."

"Gross," Dhonielle said with a giggle.

Ms. Montgomery led them into one of the two buildings that had smelled so good just a few hours ago. Now the front doors were flung open to the summer evening and the inside was aglow with light and humming with chatter. As they went, Ms. Montgomery explained that at any given time there were dozens of wolves in residence at Clawroot. They stayed for a variety of reasons ranging from pack training to long-term patrolling of Wax & Wayne to just preferring it to the outside world.

Riley hadn't thought she was hungry, but she tore through two bowls of a hearty venison stew, three buttery rolls, and just as many glasses of tea in no time at all. It was only then that she realized she hadn't eaten much since dinner the previous night.

The dining hall seemed to be in constant motion as people came in to grab their dinner, then spun out again as they finished. Riley recognized a few faces in the crowd. There were the Tenderfoot Camp teachers, Mr. Van Syckle, Mx. Green, and Ms. Song, and there were a few wolves around Darcy's age that Riley didn't know well enough to name. They all moved through the room with a sense of familiarity, laughing with each other, gathering empty bowls, sharing the work of keeping the space tidy for the next person.

An ache formed in Riley's chest. She wanted this. She wanted to be a part of *this*. She loved her family, but being a wolf changed things. It certainly had for Darcy. Before her transformation she'd been meek and quiet. A loner. But now she had her prime, and those wolves would do anything for her. She would do anything for them.

Riley wanted to know what that felt like. To be connected to four other people who really, truly cared about her.

When they'd finished eating, Ms. Montgomery took them the long way back to their cabin. On the way she pointed out various buildings and told them what they were used for. There was the Litho House, where stones were stored and prepared for important acts of lithomancy, and the Acoustics Hall, which was built in the shape of a circle and had a domed roof.

"And this"—Ms. Montgomery gestured at the building ahead—"is the archive, where the collections of nearly every pack in the alliance are stored, as well as several modern publications on wolf life and lore."

The building was easily twice the size of their cabin, and the only windows were way up high. The doors were heavy, dark wood and covered in the same scrolling wrought iron as on the Hall of Ancestors. Ms. Montgomery pushed them open to reveal a room lined with shelves and peppered with little desks.

"Oh," Dhonielle said with awe, head swiveling to take in as much as possible. All Riley saw were books, books, and more books.

"It's not as grand as a city library or anything, but we do our best. We even have a card catalog."

"Whoa. That's, like, ancient technology." Dhonielle followed at Ms. Montgomery's heels, and the rest followed Dhonielle. The room smelled like old paper and dust and just a hint of something herby like rosemary.

"I guess it is," Ms. Montgomery said, laughing lightly.

All the way in the back of the room, a figure sat hunched at a table surrounded by stacks and stacks of old books, the blue frames of her glasses just visible in the dim light.

"And look here, Bethany Books. I told you we'd find her." Ms. Montgomery smiled fondly. "All you have to do is follow the scent of obscure history, and there she'll be."

"Obscure history and magic theory," Bethany confirmed with a nod. She stood and stretched her arms with a small groan. "What brings you all to my domain?"

"Just taking a little tour before lights-out," Ms. Montgomery explained.

"I'm always glad when a tour includes the library." Bethany beamed as Dhonielle immediately began to inspect the books on her desk.

"You think a witch did this to us? Or a hunter?" Dhonielle asked, drawing her questions from the titles.

"Maybe." Bethany closed the book she'd been reading and came around the table. "But before you ask, no, I haven't found anything yet. I wish I had a better answer."

"You don't know what's wrong with us?" Aracely asked.

"There's nothing wrong with us," Riley said without thinking.

Lydia caught her eye and smiled.

"My sisters think it was the Devouring Wolf or that the Nameless Witch put a curse on us," Aracely added in a whisper.

"The good news about that is that it's completely impossible because those things don't exist," Bethany answered brightly.

"Oh." Aracely actually seemed disappointed by this answer. Riley made a note to always question Aracely's judgment.

"I won't stop looking. I promise." Bethany gestured to the piles on her desk. "I've barely gotten started. There's plenty more to learn."

Riley's stomach dropped at the sight of all those books. There had to be dozens, all piled around a single table. Most of them had the words *witches*, *hunters*, *spells*, and *snares* on them. How could one person ever sort through so much information to find the bits that mattered?

And what if the answer wasn't there at all?

For a cold second, all of Riley's fears returned. She felt certain that she would never be a real wolf. That she didn't really have anything special inside her at all.

"Hey." Bethany's voice was soft as she swept her gaze across their five faces. "Hang in there. We're going to figure this out. Because why?"

"Wolves run together," they mumbled the familiar saying.

They left the library and returned to the cabin just as the sky above turned deep purple. The moon would soon be above the trees.

"Now, pups, I want you to listen to me," Ms. Montgomery said as all five of them climbed the steps. "Clawroot is a safe place, but you must stay inside the wards."

"Why?" Riley asked automatically. "Are there really hunters out there? Are the new wolves in danger?"

"We're searching, but we don't think so. It seems that the snare Dhonielle's mom ran into was the only one. We think it might have been several years old and whatever hunter set it is long gone. Still, we just need to know where you are at all times, okay? We'll find plenty to keep you busy."

They mumbled their agreement, but just the fact that they were bound to Clawroot made Riley want to leave it again. It was what Mama N called her contrary instincts.

"Right, lights-out at nine p.m., and I'll see you for breakfast."

Ms. Montgomery left them at the door and immediately hurried off in the direction of the last cabin in the row. Inside, they took turns in the bathroom and changed into their pajamas. None of them realized how late it had gotten, and by the time they were done, it was nearly nine already.

Lydia was sitting in bed, writing in a journal, while Aracely had her earbuds in and lay with her eyes closed, feet bobbing along to her music. Dhonielle, of course, had her face in a book, and Kenver was carefully arranging their things until their little section of the room looked like an ad in a magazine. Riley didn't really know what to do, so she pulled out a small drawing pad.

Drawing had never come easily to Riley. In fact, when she was younger, she used to get too upset to finish anything. She'd break her pencils and tear the pages in half in a fit of fury, because nothing looked the way she'd imagined it would. Darcy was the one who'd helped her move past that impulse.

"Don't try for perfect," she'd said, taking the pencil and pad from Riley and beginning to sketch. "Perfect is boring. Try for something interesting."

She'd pushed the pad back to Riley. On the paper was the outline of a cat wearing a cowboy hat.

"Your turn," Darcy said. "Add something."

After a moment, Riley took the pencil and added a saddle to the cat's back. "Like that?"

"Exactly."

Darcy grinned and added a mouse to the saddle. Then Riley gave the mouse a T-shirt and a tiara and Darcy wrote *Milo* across the front of the shirt. They were both laughing by the end. The drawing was still posted on Riley's bedroom wall, and whenever she looked at it, she smiled.

She and Darcy still drew like that sometimes—smashing their drawings together, challenging each other with their additions—but mostly Riley drew on her own now.

Flipping to a new page, she started sketching an image of Maple, her orange tabby cat with one missing ear. She was shy and always hiding under something, so Riley added tall flowers on either side of her.

She was only halfway through the sketch when the lights flickered out and a thin scream filled the cabin.

The witch tricked him.

He went to her for a spell to recover his wolf, to call it forth under the light of the first full moon of summer, when wolf magic is its most wild and joyfully ferocious.

But the spell did not work as expected. Instead of pulling the wolf from within, it reached out, using that perfect connection between him and his prime and violently ripping their wolves away. Tearing their magic up from the roots and planting it inside him.

When it was done, his prime was dead. Their magic was his. Their ghosts were whispers in his mind. He became mad and powerful all at once. Hungry for more and heedless of where it came from.

But the witch's spell did something else.

As it increased his power beyond imagining, it also created us.

Those with the wolves that stay within.

11

LITHOCHARMS

Riley blinked at the sudden dark. The scream had ended in a series of familiar whimpers. Dhonielle really hated the dark.

"Hello?" Aracely called. "What's happening? Are we under attack?"

"Attack? From what?!" Kenver asked.

"Hunters! Witches! I don't know. The Devouring Wolf!" Aracely shouted.

"Why did you have to say that?" Dhonielle muttered weakly.

"It was just Dhonielle," Riley said, trying to restore some order to the room.

"Why would you turn the lights out?" Aracely asked.

"Not the lights. The scream," Dhonielle admitted.

"Then who shut off the lights?! If someone out there is trying to freak us out, I will fight you in the face!" Aracely shouted.

"Fight you in the face?" Riley asked.

"It's nine p.m.," Lydia explained in a calm voice. "Lights-out."

"They timed them?" Aracely asked, offended. "What happens if I have to use the bathroom? Which I do, by the way."

"How do you usually find the bathroom at night?" Kenver huffed grumpily.

"I'm pretty sure they're just litholights. All you have to do is touch the switch," Lydia said.

There was a *thump* and then an "Oof!" and then the lights came on. Aracely was standing by the bedroom door, fingers pressed to the small stone set into the wall. Litholights glowed from the ceiling in a ring, glittery granite stones that filled the room with warm light.

"Thank you," Dhonielle murmured. She was sitting in her bed with her knees drawn up, arms wrapped tightly around them. "Does anyone mind if we leave the bathroom lights on at night?"

"Wait, are you afraid of the dark?" Aracely asked.

Riley nodded along with Dhonielle. The few times Dhonielle had stayed the night they'd had to put nightlights in Riley's room and leave the light on in the bathroom all night. Milo still needed a nightlight, but Riley hadn't used them since she was at least nine.

"That's easy," Aracely said, bouncing back. Even her sleep shirt was covered in little rainbow-colored dinosaurs.

She dug around in her top drawer and came out with a velvet purple pouch that clattered and clinked when she shook it. She untied the cord, then dumped the contents onto her bedspread. They were crystals in every color. Pink and blue and yellow, even one that was a dark, swirly green. Everyone crowded around for a closer look.

"Here, this one's light." Aracely selected a yellow one and tossed it to Dhonielle. "It's not so bright that it'll bother anyone, and you can keep it with you even when you have to pee."

Dhonielle tapped the stone with her index finger and it began to glow in the palm of her hand. It reminded Riley of a firefly except it was the size of a walnut.

"Thank you." Dhonielle smiled with her whole face.

"What do the others do?" Riley asked.

"Oh, you know, this and that," Aracely said breezily. She selected a blue one and tossed it to Lydia. "This one sounds like the ocean if you hold it up to your ear." She plucked a clear crystal and handed it to Riley. "This one is like the light one except it makes shadows." She volleyed a pink one to Kenver. "This one smells good. I usually leave it in the bathroom because, like I said, sisters are smelly."

"Lithocharms! Did you make these?" Lydia asked.

"Yep. It's pretty easy once you get the hang of it. Mx. Green said it was okay as long as I never took them to school or anything, which, I don't really know why that would matter. People never look at something and expect magic. They're just a bunch of rocks!" She paused thought-fully. "I guess there was that one time I nailed Grant Shipley with one, but he deserved it."

The charm in Riley's hand was about the size of a quar-ter. It reminded her of the grape she'd put inside the stone just before the Full Moon Rite. The growl had distracted her so much that she'd almost forgotten she'd done it.

This stone hummed lightly against her skin. To someone who wasn't used to magic it would just feel a little warm, but she could feel the vibration of Aracely's spell. Most lithocharms were small like this, but great lithomages could shape whole buildings from boulders.

Riley rubbed her thumb over the crystal's smooth face and imagined shadows. At once, a dark cloud settled over her. It was as though someone had dimmed the lights, except Riley could see *through* the shadows.

"Whoa," Kenver said, peering at Riley. "That's amaz-ing. I can hardly see her anymore."

"I guess," Aracely said with a shrug. "I mostly use that one to hide from my little sister, Sara. She doesn't really understand what personal space means."

Riley rubbed her thumb across the crystal again and the shadows dropped away. Lithocharms were common and relatively straightforward. They all learned how to make them at camp, but some people were just better at it than others. Aracely clearly had a talent for it.

"Oh, I like this one," Lydia said, holding the blue

crystal to her ear. "The ocean sound is so soothing."

"Yeah, I use that one to sleep sometimes. Like last night. I heard this weird growling noise. It woke me up, so I stuck that one in my pillow, and then I slept like the dead," Aracely said, nodding her head.

"A growl?" Riley asked, suddenly alert.

"Yeah, like a wolf sound, but not? Anyway, I imagine things all the time, that's what my mom says, but this was just so loud I had to do something."

Dhonielle shifted nervously on her feet. Kenver stared wide-eyed at Aracely, and even Lydia seemed unnerved by Aracely's confession.

"Why are you all looking at me?" Aracely asked. Her hands flew to her mouth. "What did I say? Do I have something stuck in my teeth?!"

"I heard a growl, too," Riley said. "I've heard it twice. The first time was the day of the Full Moon Rite and the second time was late last night."

"I heard it, too." Dhonielle's eyebrows were climbing up her forehead.

"Me, too," Lydia said.

They all turned to Kenver, who was standing back from the group, one arm pulled protectively across their stomach.

They nodded. "I heard it. Same times as Riley said."

"What do you think it means?" Dhonielle asked.

For a moment they stood in a silent circle, each

looking to the next for answers none of them had.

"I don't know," Riley admitted. "Again."

"Feels like there's an awful lot we don't know." Lydia blew at a strand of her blond hair. "Or maybe just a lot the adults aren't telling us."

"Maybe it's too terrible and they don't want to tell us?" Dhonielle suggested.

Kenver rolled their eyes and added, "If they even care that much."

"What are you talking about? Of course they care! They care, and they're working on it. We just have to be patient," Aracely explained.

"Weren't you the one sobbing your eyes out last night?" Kenver asked. "Why are you suddenly so relaxed about things?"

"I was upset last night. It was so surprising! But I'm sure everything is going to work out fine." Aracely blinked her big brown eyes at Kenver, who scowled in return.

"That seems pretty naive, if you ask me," Kenver grumbled.

"I didn't," Aracely answered airly, as though Kenver's dark mood were completely irrelevant.

"So," Riley said, breaking the tension that was starting to thicken in the room. "If we want to get to the bottom of things, I think we should start with Bethany's books."

"Bethany Books's books," Aracely said with a laugh. "Get it?"

"Do you think they'll let us?" Dhonielle asked.

"I don't think she means we should ask permission." Lydia tipped a smile toward Dhonielle.

"Sneak out?!" Dhonielle squeaked. "No, we can't do that. I don't want to get in trouble. I'll wait here."

Riley considered leaving Dhonielle behind. She was actually pretty terrible at being sneaky and she was unlikely to tell on them, but she was also the most bookish person Riley knew. Even here, she'd arrived with a stack of books that now sat on her bedside table.

"Please, Dhonielle? You will be so much better at sorting through all of those old books. We need your help."

Dhonielle made a face that was halfway between a smile and squint with her nose all crinkled up. "I don't want to get caught," she insisted.

"Because that's the worst thing that could happen to us this week." Kenver raised their camera and randomly snapped a picture of the corner.

"We won't," Riley promised. "We'll be fast and careful, and even if we do get caught, I'll take the blame. Okay?"

"Okay." Dhonielle heaved a sigh.

Riley grinned, then looked at the others as she thought through the plan. Leaders always needed to start with Rule #1.

"We'll go just after midnight. Dhonielle will be our researcher. Aracely, you bring those lithocharms—the light and shadows in particular. And, Lydia, can you bring your journal to take notes?"

"Sure," Lydia said with a bob of her head.

"Perfect." Riley beamed.

"What about me?" Kenver asked.

Riley was caught off guard. She hadn't realized that she'd given everyone a task except for Kenver.

"Oh, well, you can . . . take pictures?" Riley knew it was a miss before she'd even finished saying it.

"Pictures?" Kenver gave Riley a withering look. "Of what, exactly?"

"Of . . . the . . . books?"

Lydia stepped in before Riley could make things worse. "Why don't you be the lookout, okay? We'll need one."

"Sure," Kenver said with a shrug.

Riley wished she'd been the one to think of it. It seemed so obvious now that Lydia had once again stepped into the middle of Riley's plan to make it better.

"Great," Lydia said brightly, flashing a perfect smile at Riley.

"Great," Riley repeated, flashing a not-smile in return. "Everyone get some sleep and be ready to go at midnight," she said in the same way Mama C would have issued an order to the pack.

They climbed back into bed, and just before the lights flickered out again, Dhonielle murmured, "I hate the dark."

12

WHO'S AFRAID OF THE BIG BAD WOLF?

Riley was asleep the second her head hit the pillow. Not even the excitement of sneaking out in a few hours could keep her awake. It wasn't until she heard people shuffling around the cabin that she opened her eyes.

A small light glowed in the room, turning everyone into ghostly shapes in the dark. They moved around, whispering softly. It sent a shiver down Riley's spine until there was a familiar *thump* and an "Oof!"

"Dhonielle, can you shine that light over here? I think there's a spider in my boot," Aracely said.

Instead of moving her light charm in Aracely's direction, Dhonielle shrieked and dropped it on the floor. Aracely scooped it up and aimed it into her shoe.

"Oh! Never mind. It's just a scrunchie." She tugged a

bright purple scrunchie from the inside of her boot and held it up proudly.

"Everyone ready?" Lydia asked.

Riley was out of bed in a second. She tugged her jean jacket over her shoulders and stuffed her feet into her own boots, hoping that there were no spiders inside them.

"Dhonielle," she whispered. "You can have the charm, but you can't use it when we're outside."

Dhonielle clutched the light to her chest. Her braids were puffy on either side of her head, her face a narrow slash of warm brown in the light.

"Are you sure you need me? Maybe I should just stay here," she suggested.

Riley did her best not to frown at her cousin, but Aracely looped an arm through Dhonielle's and nudged her with one hip. "We totally need you. I can read like five words before I start to fall asleep, and everyone else has a job. Lydia has to take notes, Kenver has to keep watch, and Riley has to keep us all on task. I'll make it my job to keep you company, okay?"

"Okay," Dhonielle said, sounding like it was not okay at all, but she extinguished the light and followed the group out of the bedroom.

"Remember, it's a full moon," Riley whispered, an excited feeling tingling all the way down to her toes.

"Stick to the shadows as much as possible so we don't get caught."

With that, she carefully opened the door and took a peek outside. Lights glowed softly in the windows of the cabin next door. In the sky above, the moon was still full and round, painting Clawroot in silver light surrounded by inky shadows. It was the best and worst of both worlds: enough light to see or be seen. After a minute passed with no sign of adults on the prowl, Riley opened the door a little wider and slipped onto the porch.

She was about to give the all-clear sign when she heard the sound of another door opening. Instinctively, Riley dropped into the bushes, hiding just in time for two figures to emerge from the last cabin in the row. She recognized them at once: Bethany Books and Mama C.

They were too far away to hear, but Bethany gestured repeatedly with her hands, pointing back inside the cabin. Mama C shook her head. Whatever Bethany was suggesting, Mama C didn't agree. They looked upset.

Riley barely dared to breathe. If her mom caught her sneaking out on her first night in Clawroot, she would be in so much trouble. But why was Mama C still here, anyway? And what were they fighting about?

"Riley!" Lydia's whisper was a hiss.

Riley peered over the edge of the porch. Only one of Lydia's eyes was visible through a narrow crack in the door. Riley held up a hand, telling Lydia to wait.

After another minute, Bethany went back inside the cabin and Riley's mom left. Riley watched long enough to make sure she wasn't headed toward the archive—which would render her entire plan pointless!—then crawled out of the bushes.

"Hurry!" Riley whispered, gesturing for the others to follow.

Once they were all together, the night felt both inviting and dangerous.

The archive wasn't too far away, but they had to cross a few wide-open spaces to reach it. The full moon turned everything into islands of light and puddles of shadow. Riley hurried her group from shadow to shadow, pausing at each to check for signs of trouble.

As promised, Aracely never let go of Dhonielle's hand, and Dhonielle only whimpered in fear twice. Lydia ran at Riley's side, matching her pace, while Kenver darted out in front, making sure the way was clear. They reached the archive doors first.

"It's locked," Kenver hissed.

"Does anybody know how to pick a lock?" Riley asked.

"Sure, but I need a screwdriver and a hammer," Aracely answered with a shrug.

All four of them turned to stare at her.

"What? It works!"

"I can do it," Dhonielle said.

"You can?" Riley asked in surprise. "How?"

"With my call," Dhonielle explained.

Riley had never heard Dhonielle use her call in anything above a polite speaking volume. She couldn't imagine Dhonielle was strong enough to push a shrub out of her path, much less crack a lock. Then again, her scream was piercing.

"Give it a shot," Lydia said.

With a shrug, Dhonielle moved forward and cupped the knob in both hands. She leaned in and howled very quietly. The hair on Riley's neck prickled the way it always did around acoustic magic. Before she could worry that the sound would draw attention, something clicked.

Dhonielle stood up and twisted the knob. The door swung open.

"That," Aracely said, sounding impressed, "was better than my method."

"It's easy, really," Dhonielle said. "Just takes a little practice. I can teach you if you want."

"Yep, I want," Aracely replied, following the rest of the group inside. "That would be great for getting inside my sister's room when she steals my stuff. Or for getting inside the house when I forget my keys."

Riley quickly and quietly shut the door behind them, plunging the room into full darkness.

"Oh no. Oh no. Oh no," Dhonielle whispered frantically.

The only windows were too far up the walls to admit

much light. Definitely not enough to read by.

"Dhonielle," Riley whispered. "Now you can use the charm."

For a second there was no response, then a small cloud of light appeared in Dhonielle's hands. Her eyes were wide with fear, but that changed as the light slowly spread and illuminated the library. It looked even bigger than it had in daylight. Books upon books upon books.

"Wow," Dhonielle gasped.

"Whoa," Riley said at the same time.

They needed a plan.

"So what exactly am I looking for?" Dhonielle asked.

Riley had been asking herself the same question. The adults were already investigating, so they should start with something the adults didn't know about: the growl. They'd all heard it on the day of the Full Moon Rite, then again later that same night. They hadn't imagined it, which meant it was magic. Wolf magic. Then there was the fact that they were technically still tenderfoot pups. It wasn't much, but maybe it was enough.

"What about books on the magic of tenderfoot pups?" Riley asked.

"You could also look for things about magical ailments and inhibitions or maybe even infections," Kenver added thoughtfully. "Magic is one of the systems in our bodies. Like the respiratory system or the circulatory system.

Except instead of lungs or blood, it's magic. So if something is wrong with a part of the system, something might be wrong with all of it."

They all stared at Kenver.

"You sound like a teacher," Lydia said in awe.

Kenver blushed and shrugged, then quickly remembered to scowl. "I like magic."

"So do I, but it's magic." Aracely waved a hand through the air. "It doesn't make much sense because it's all—what's the word? The *E* word?"

"Energy?" Lydia suggested. "Enigmatic?"

"Elusive? Electric? Effective?" Riley added.

"No, nope, uh-uh." Aracely tapped her bottom lip, still searching for the right word.

"Ethereal," Dhonielle said.

"Yeah! That's the one. Magic is ethereal," Aracely finished.

Kenver tipped their head to one side as they thought. "I guess I don't like feeling like something inside me can work or do things that I don't understand. Magic isn't just . . ." Kenver waved a hand in the air for dramatic effect. "Magic. It has rules and everything. It only feels ethereal because it's been a part of you forever. You don't think about breathing, do you?"

"Only when my sisters sit on me," Aracely answered seriously.

Now they all stared at Aracely.

"What? What did I say?"

"Nothing," Riley said with a shake of her head. "Ready, Dhonielle?"

Dhonielle nodded enthusiastically. "Ready."

Being around so many books seemed to drive all of Dhonielle's fear away. She started with the books on Bethany's table, sorting through them as easily as if she were searching for her favorite kind of candy. Then she moved on to the stacks. Her fingers danced over spines, occasionally pulling one free to page through the contents and returning each to its spot with care when she was done.

Lydia perched nearby, ready to make notes, while Kenver stayed by the front doors to keep watch and Riley did her best to help look through Bethany's books. The topics covered everything from preadolescent werewolf development to the history of the True North Wolfpack, who still existed and had some truly archaic ideas about who could and couldn't be a wolf. They especially didn't like families like hers with Moon Bite wolves. The idea that they might have something to do with what was happening made Riley's stomach curdle.

After fifteen minutes passed without a word, Aracely huffed and slammed the book she'd been paging through.

"This one is just blank! Who puts a blank book in a library?! I really wish this kind of wolf stuff was on the internet. You know. So it was searchable? Do you think this place has any books on dinosaurs? No, never mind. I know the answer to that," she said. "I'm just going to sit over here, and you tell me when you have something I need to look at."

Then, true to her word, Aracely sat down next to Dhonielle and popped her earbuds into her ears.

Riley understood her frustration. The task seemed insurmountable and she was getting tired. There had to be an answer somewhere in this room, but it was starting to feel like it would be in the very last book they opened.

With a sigh, Riley decided to change tactics and pull a book called *Practical Transformations* from the bottom of one stack. The cover was a dingy red with the title written in letters that once must have been gold but were now brown. The pages were soft and tattered at the edges, and as Riley leafed through, she found a bookmark stuck near the end on a chapter titled "The Summoning Rite: Calling Forth the Wolf."

Riley bent closer, reading quickly. It was a guide for a rite that was specifically meant to help someone transform into a wolf! And it seemed fairly straightforward. All they had to do was find something called "the heart of wolves" and then focus their calling magic on the afflicted person. It seemed so easy!

"Lydia!" Riley thrust the book into Lydia's hands. "Copy this page."

"What is it?" Lydia peered curiously at the text, eyes widening as she realized what she was looking at. "You think this could work?"

"Had to be on Bethany's desk for a reason, right?" Riley answered.

With a nod, Lydia started dutifully copying the page into her journal.

"Hmm," Dhonielle said, breaking into Riley's thoughts. "I don't see anything specific about hearing growls like we did, but look at this."

She pushed a large tome toward Riley.

"It's about the Devouring Wolf," she explained.

Without meaning to, Riley thought of Milo and how irritating he'd been the night of the first full moon. And how easy it had been to scare him with the old story. Her irritation seemed so unimportant now.

Riley sighed. "Dhonielle. We're supposed to be looking for information, not mythology."

"I know, I know, but I've never seen this version before."

"What's different about it?" Riley asked.

"Well, this one says that when the Devourer rose, there were some tenderfoot pups who didn't transform."

"Wait. Are you saying . . ." Lydia closed her journal and leaned in, but she couldn't finish the thought.

For a moment, they could only stare at each other in horrified silence. Every story they'd ever heard or told about the Devouring Wolf was suddenly more terrifying that it had ever been before. But it was the last thing Dhonielle had said that Riley couldn't shake.

Turning to face her cousin, she asked, "How many tenderfoot pups?"

Dhonielle's eyes widened as she looked from Riley to the others. "Five."

There were five of us at the start. Five who did not transform during the Moon Rite. We were left behind like saplings in a forest of giants. That's how we thought of ourselves, as saplings. We had no idea how apt a name it was. Saplings may not appear very strong. They are small and weedy, and haven't yet had time for their roots to dig in deep. One sharp tug is all it takes to pluck them from the earth. Yet their frailty is also their strength. For as they bend and twist, they withstand winds capable of breaking even the oldest of oaks.

If we had figured that out sooner, maybe we could have stopped some of the terrible things that happened.

It is my greatest hope that by reading this, you will not only defeat him for good, but you will all survive.

13

EEE! SHH! WHOOPS.

After returning every book to its spot and the chairs to their proper places, they left the archive behind.

This time, the night didn't feel as exciting as it had when they'd first left the cabin. It felt darker and thicker. It felt like something was watching them from behind opaque windows, waiting to leap out from behind bushes or around buildings.

They went as fast as possible, hurrying from one shadow to the next. They were eager to get back to the safety of their beds where they could burrow into soft blankets and try to forget everything they'd ever heard about the Devouring Wolf.

An owl sang overhead, startling an "Eee!" from Dhonielle.

"Shhh!" Kenver and Aracely said together.

Riley's heart jumped into her throat. She barely contained her own cry of surprise. Dhonielle clasped both hands over her mouth and breathed heavily through her nose.

Lydia tugged all three of them deeper into the shadow of the nearest building while Riley searched for any sign that they'd been heard. But the night was eerily still and quiet. So quiet, Riley almost didn't want to move again.

But if they didn't move, they'd never get back.

Together, they darted through moonlight to the next building, then paused to wait and watch.

The owl called again. This time Dhonielle clasped her hand over her mouth before she could make a noise. Aracely patted her approvingly on the shoulder.

Dhonielle dropped her hands and whispered, "I hate this."

"You're doing great," Aracely whispered back. She gave Dhonielle a big smile.

"What was that?" Kenver hissed.

They peered behind them, eyebrows furrowed as they listened to something no one else could hear.

Riley stepped closer. "What?"

"I don't know," Kenver said. "It's gone now."

"Please don't be teasing us," Dhonielle whimpered.

"I'm not teasing you. I thought I heard something. Voices," Kenver said, then shook their head. "But not anymore."

"Let's keep moving," Riley said, taking the lead, but

they'd only gone a few feet when the sound of voices stopped them in their tracks.

Riley spun on her heel, gesturing tightly for the others to go back, go back, go back!

They crashed together, all five of them diving into the narrow space between the bushes and the building. They crouched down and kept as still as possible as two figures appeared.

"You shouldn't be here," said a voice that Riley knew all too well. "I thought I made that clear."

Mama C stepped into the moonlight followed by a slender wolf. The wolf slowed and began to shimmer, transforming into their human body.

"It's not up to you, is it?"

Dhonielle inhaled sharply at the voice.

Aunt Alexis was dressed in loose-fitting linen pants and a tank top that showed off the muscles in her arms. Her hair was tied back in a puffed bun and her silver cuff gleamed at her wrist. She narrowed her eyes at Mama C.

"I think it is," Mama C said, stepping closer to Aunt Alexis. "You aren't well. That hunters' snare did a number on you, and you need to recuperate."

"A snare." Aunt Alexis's voice was cold. "And how did it get there? The South Wood has been clear for years."

Mama C frowned. "I've told you already, I don't know. But I will find out, and in the meantime, you should rest."

Aunt Alexis looked like she didn't believe anything Mama C was saying. She crossed her arms over her chest and glared.

"Please," Mama C continued. "I'm worried about you."

Something subtle passed between them then and Aunt Alexis laughed softly with a shake of her head. "Right," she said.

"Why are they fighting?" Dhonielle breathed so quietly, Riley almost didn't hear her.

Riley could only shake her head. She'd known her mom and Aunt Alexis to argue, as siblings often did, but this felt different. This felt like a wolf resisting their alpha, and she had no idea what would have inspired Aunt Alexis to behave this way.

"Then what are *you* doing here?" Aunt Alexis demanded.

"Keeping an eye on things," Mama C answered calmly.

Aunt Alexis began backing away slowly.

"That makes two of us." She said it like it was a threat.

Mama C stood in the moonlight, fingers curling into loose fists at her sides as Aunt Alexis disappeared into the woods. When she was gone, Mama C took one step down the path that led to their cabin by the stream. Riley stiffened, worried that she was going to find them missing before they could return. Then, all of a sudden, Mama C changed directions, hurrying into the woods after Aunt Alexis.

For several long minutes, none of them moved. Finally, Aracely whispered, "Dhonielle, can you please get off my foot?"

"Sorry, sorry."

Slowly, they picked their way from the bushes. Something about having been so close to Mama C and Aunt Alexis left Riley feeling much more exposed than before. The excitement she'd felt at the start of their outing had vanished, and now all she wanted to do was get back to their cabin.

Her mind was flooded with questions. Why was Mama C still here? Why was Aunt Alexis still here, for that matter? And why had there been so much tension between them? It seemed like Aunt Alexis blamed Mama C for the hunters' snare, but why? Aunt Alexis had been acting strange at the cabin this morning, too. Had the snare injured her more than they knew?

And why were they out lurking on the grounds this late?

Riley didn't have any answers, and she didn't think she was likely to get them even if she asked. Besides, asking would mean revealing that she'd been out of her cabin when she shouldn't be, so that wasn't an option.

She was so consumed with her thoughts that she didn't realize she'd started walking back to the cabin on her own until she heard someone calling her name. Loudly.

"Riley! Wait!" Aracely's voice could wake the dead and probably had.

"Shhhh!" Riley spun around with both hands raised. Aracely and Dhonielle were running to catch up, with Lydia and Kenver a few paces behind. "Aracely Bravo, do you want to get cau—"

Riley stopped midsentence at the sight of Kenver clutching a book to their chest.

"Kenver, did you take a book from the archive?"

Kenver shrugged as though it didn't matter, which it most certainly did.

"You stole a book?!" Dhonielle's voice was louder than it needed to be.

"Why?" Aracely seemed genuinely confused by this turn of events. To be fair, Riley was, too.

"Shhhh!" Riley urged again.

"Because I felt like it," Kenver answered with a stubborn scowl. "Besides, it's blank, it didn't belong there in the first place."

"You don't know that!" Riley couldn't believe what she was hearing. "What if someone misses it?"

"Who would miss an empty book?" Kenver's arms tightened around the stolen prize.

"Maybe we should have this conversation inside?" Lydia suggested. "They probably heard Aracely all the way at Tenderfoot Camp."

"Hey!" Aracely's response was not soft. "I'm not the one who stole the book."

"And I'm not the one who can't whisper!" Kenver sniped back.

"Friends?" Lydia asked.

"We're taking the book back right now," Riley said decisively. "Let's go."

"Uuugh," said Aracely. "You're not the boss of me."

"Why don't we do it in the morning? We can do it first thing. Bethany will never know it was missing," Dhonielle suggested with a nervous glance toward the archive. Taking it back now would mean another risky trip across Clawroot, and it was already late.

"Who said I'm giving it back?"

Riley could not figure out why Kenver had taken the book in the first place, much less why they were so committed to keeping it.

"Hey, friends!" Lydia all but shouted.

Everyone turned to Lydia and said, "SHHH!"

Lydia raised a finger and pointed to a figure standing a few feet away, a long shawl wrapped around her shoulders and bright blue glasses gleaming in the moonlight.

"I think she'll notice," Lydia said.

Riley froze. Her blood went cold and her heart skipped a whole beat as her brain hissed, *Caught!*

"Oh, great!" Aracely flung her hands into the air, then

rounded on Lydia. "You could have said something sooner!"

"I . . ." Lydia folded her arms across her stomach. "I did."

"We're in trouble," Dhonielle hissed, shooting an accusing look at Riley.

Bethany clapped three times. It was so startling that they all stopped talking and looked at her. "Thank you," she said. "I assume I don't have to explain the kind of trouble you're in?"

"This much?" Aracely held her thumb and forefinger about an inch apart.

Bethany only shook her head.

"It's too late to discuss right now, and you should have been asleep hours ago. But since you're all so eager to be *out* of bed, you can get up bright and early. I expect to see you on your porch no later than six a.m., understood?"

"Understood," they answered wearily, trudging up the steps.

Riley felt heavy as she shut the cabin door behind them. One day in Clawroot and they were already in trouble. She didn't want to imagine what Mama C would think when she heard they'd snuck out at the first opportunity. To make matters worse, they hadn't even learned anything valuable. It had been a wasted effort from start to finish.

Just before the lights went out, Riley noticed the stolen book sitting on Kenver's nightstand. It looked more like a journal than a book, with a chocolatey leather cover embossed with the letters *G. B.* No, not just letters. Initials. It *did* belong to someone. Which meant it would definitely be missed.

Riley pinched her eyes shut and tried to ignore the little flutter of panic in her chest. First thing tomorrow, they'd take it back. Hopefully before it could cause them any more trouble.

14

DOUBLE TROUBLE

Morning arrived way too soon. The sky was still dim with dawn when Riley peeled her eyes open. Aracely was humming like nothing was wrong as she breezed out of the bathroom in a cloud of coconut-and-jasmine scent. Somehow she'd managed to get up not only before the very last minute, but early enough to get a hot shower.

"Bathroom's free," she sang as she squeezed her wet curls in a small towel. Not even the promise of a day filled with consequences could get her down.

"But we're not." Kenver was already in a bad mood. They spared a dark look for Riley, then added, "Nice of you to join us."

"I can't believe this. I just can't believe this." Dhonielle sounded miserable. She probably was. She could probably count on one hand the number of times she'd ever broken a rule before.

"You better hurry up." Lydia was pulling her hair up

into a perfect little ponytail. She was already dressed and ready to go.

Riley blinked her heavy lids and slowly dragged herself up to sitting. "What time is it?" she asked.

"It's five fifty-four in the *morning,*" Aracely answered.

Instantly, Riley was up, heart pounding as she brushed her teeth faster than ever before in her life. She tried to ignore the fact that no one had bothered to wake her up. Were they just going to let her sleep her way into even bigger trouble? They must be more upset about last night than she'd realized. But none of that had been her fault, so why did it feel like they blamed her?

By the time she'd dressed and dashed onto the front porch, it was five after six. Bethany was waiting, and she wasn't alone.

Riley groaned inwardly at the sight of Mama C standing with her arms crossed and a look of disappointment on her face.

"You're late," Bethany said.

The others avoided looking at her. Which was fine with Riley. She wasn't feeling very much like eye contact at the moment.

"Sorry," Riley mumbled.

"Now you'll only have fifteen minutes for breakfast instead of twenty before we begin." Bethany shrugged as the others groaned. Riley could practically feel them blaming her.

"Sorry," she mumbled again.

"Okay, pups, let's get moving." Bethany turned to lead the group toward breakfast.

"Riley." With a single tip of her head, Mama C made Riley's name a command.

The air was already sticky with humidity as Riley followed her mom into dew-soaked grass. She knew she was in trouble. They were all in trouble. But it didn't seem fair that she was in even more trouble simply because she was the daughter of Great Callahan.

Riley's stomach growled as the others shuffled toward the dining hall, leaving Riley alone with her mom and that disappointed expression.

"I'm sorry!" Riley blurted. Sometimes aggressive apologizing was the fastest way to a resolution. Which, in this case, included breakfast.

Mama C studied Riley without speaking.

Riley kept going. "I know we shouldn't have snuck out, but we weren't doing anything *bad*. We went to the archive, and it's only because no one will tell us anything and because we all heard this weird growl on the night of the first full moon, so we were trying to find out if it was connected."

"What do you mean you heard a growl?" Mama C asked.

"We heard a growl, and it was like it was in our heads. I heard one in the backyard before we left for the Full

Moon Rite and I thought I'd imagined it, but then the others heard one, too!" Riley felt more confident now. They'd had a good reason for sneaking out after all. "We went to the archive to look it up."

"And what did you learn?" Mama C asked.

"Um. Well." Riley hesitated. *Nothing* didn't sound like a very impressive answer.

"We don't want to get your hopes up before we have something to share with you, do you understand that? We aren't keeping things from you, Riley, but you can't help because you're not—" Mama C stopped herself suddenly.

Real wolves, whispered a voice in Riley's head.

"We're doing the best we can, and I thought I could trust you to keep the group calm while we work." Mama C didn't sound mad, she sounded a little bit sad, which was worse. "Can I trust you to do that in the future? Keep them calm and follow the rules?"

Rules were deeply important to Mama C. Breaking them was rarely, if ever, tolerated, but even she had to agree that these were extreme circumstances. The problem was simply too big for the usual rules.

That wasn't what Mama C wanted to hear, of course.

Riley opened her mouth to answer when a muffled cry rose from the cabin at the end of the row. The same one Mama C and Bethany had argued in front of last night.

Mama C turned sharp eyes toward the sound.

"I have to go," she said.

"Who was that?" Riley asked, following her mom's gaze.

"No one. You don't need to worry about it." Her mom took her by the shoulders and started to turn her away, then stopped. "Actually, I do need you to worry about it."

"Okay." A thrilling mixture of fear and excitement stirred in Riley's stomach.

"I cannot tell you everything that is happening right now, but there is something in the woods. Something dangerous. I need you to keep a clear head and make sure the others don't go wandering off. I need you to keep them calm and safe. Can you do that?" Mama C's hands were firm on Riley's shoulders. Great Leader Callahan needed her help.

"You can trust me," Riley promised. "Rule Number Four, right? Do the tough stuff."

Mama C blinked, then nodded. "Exactly. And if you notice anything strange, anything at all, come tell me at once."

Warmth expanded in Riley's chest. She had a mission, a task from Great Callahan herself. And she would not fail. "I promise," she said brightly. Then she turned and ran all the way to breakfast.

15

ALPHA

Riley reached the dining hall in time to shove a bagel in her mouth and wash it down with some orange juice before Bethany announced it was time to go.

They left the dining hall and headed south. The carefully manicured stone pathways of the main village fell away until they were traipsing through a wild and weedy field. The sun was still inching its way into the sky, and the tall grass was heavy with dew that soaked Riley's jeans up to the thighs.

"I didn't realize Clawroot was this big," Kenver said when they'd been walking for a while. They were dressed for the hike, with a plain black shirt beneath an orange-and-blue-plaid shirt, and black jeans tucked into work boots.

"The Hall of Ancestors looks so small from here." Aracely had paused to squint back over her shoulder. Her curly hair was wrapped up into two tight buns on top of her head like bows. "And I can't even see our cabin."

"There are one hundred and two acres in Clawroot," Bethany called from several yards ahead of them. "Keep up, pups!"

They trudged up and down small hills, in and out of fields thick with summer grasses. They even hopped over a stream. The sun peered over the trees, promising to turn all the cool dew on the grass into sticky humidity.

As they walked, Riley's mind wandered through all that had happened last night. From the story they'd found about the five tenderfoot pups who didn't transform when the Devouring Wolf rose up to the argument they'd witnessed between Mama C and Aunt Alexis to her mother's warning that something was in the woods. It all seemed connected, but she couldn't puzzle out how. Whatever it was must have something to do with what had happened to Aunt Alexis, and Riley was beginning to suspect that it all added up to something even more dangerous than a hunters' snare.

"I'm so hot," Kenver whined softly.

Riley knew how they felt. It was sweltering out here, and she had at least four bug bites on her arms already.

"So much for my shower," Aracely said. "I'm sweating so much, I'm basically a fish."

"That doesn't make sense," Kenver responded.

"Of course it does. Fish are wet and so am I," Aracely explained. "I'd rather be a bird, though."

"So you could fly?" Lydia asked.

"No! I mean, sure. That would be cool. Maybe a little scary."

"You're a werewolf and you think being a bird sounds scary?" Lydia was smiling.

"I like having my feet on the ground, thank you very much." Aracely raised her chin haughtily.

"Then why would you like to be a bird?" Kenver asked, returning to the point of the original question.

"Because they're dinosaurs and dinosaurs are super-cool." She paused. "Dinosaurs never sweat."

Riley felt like an outsider listening to their easy conversation. She was still upset with them for not waking her up this morning and didn't know what to do about it. She had to do something, though. She had a job to do, from Great Callahan herself, and she couldn't do it if she was nursing hurt feelings.

"We never should have snuck out," Dhonielle said with a sigh.

"Yeah," Aracely agreed. "That was not a good idea."

Riley waited for Lydia or Kenver to disagree, but neither of them did.

"It wasn't the sneaking out that got us into trouble," Riley countered. "It was getting caught."

Dhonielle huffed and shook her head. "That's not how that works, you know. It's cause and effect, not effect only."

It was hard to argue with that. If they hadn't snuck

out, then they wouldn't be here now. As much as Riley didn't want to take the blame, this was a moment for Rule #4: *Do the tough stuff.*

"You're right. We only got caught because we were out in the first place. I'm sorry about that." She swiped at the tall grass bending across the path in front of her.

"We didn't even learn anything." Dhonielle sounded utterly tragic. Like they were talking about her dog dying instead of getting caught sneaking around a very safe, highly protected werewolf village. "We're in trouble for nothing."

She was right. Riley had been so sure they would learn something new. Something that could help them. And instead they'd come away with nothing to show for it. She'd failed.

"We learned about those other five tenderfoot pups," Aracely offered.

"That was just a story, Aracely." Kenver used the sleeve of their flannel to mop up the sweat on their forehead. Their cheeks were turning bright pink and they were scowling harder than usual. "Can't you tell the difference between real and fake?"

"Of course I can," Aracely protested. "I can also tell the difference between what's mine and what I shouldn't steal from a library. Unlike *some* people."

"At least I know when to keep my voice down," Kenver sniped. "Unlike *you.*"

"Well, at least I'm not sulking around like a grumpy potato!"

"Oh, come on, don't fight." Lydia stepped between the two of them before Kenver could say anything else. "Let's just get through this so we can do what we should have done in the first place and wait for the adults to figure this out."

Lydia hadn't been looking at Riley when she said it, but Riley knew it was aimed at her. Just like she knew this was her fault. And real leaders, real alphas, owned their mistakes.

Kenver looked like they were ready to say more, but Riley spoke up first.

"Lydia's right. You all wait here," she said, coming to a decision. "I'm going to go talk to Bethany."

"About what?" Dhonielle asked.

"I'm going to tell her that I was responsible and I'm the only one who should be punished. Whatever the punishment is, I'll do it alone."

"You can't do that," Lydia said.

"Why?" Riley thought they would be happy that she was ready to take the blame, but Lydia wasn't the only one scowling at her now. Kenver was, which didn't really mean anything, but so were Aracely and Dhonielle.

"Because you can't make decisions for us," Lydia answered sharply. "It's not like you're our alpha."

Riley felt as though she'd been punched in the gut. She

hadn't even had a chance to become an alpha and now Lydia was telling her she couldn't be one.

"I know." Riley almost couldn't say the words out loud. She felt sick all of a sudden.

"Only wolves have alphas," Dhonielle added.

"And we're not wolves," Aracely finished.

No one said anything after that. A heavy silence swelled between them until Riley was almost convinced she could drown in it.

Aracely was right. They weren't wolves. And it was starting to seem like they might never be. Riley's stomach twisted hard at the thought. She missed her friends. She missed Stacey, but would Stacey ever want to talk to her again if she never became a real wolf?

Then Kenver sighed.

"I really wanted to turn into a wolf that night." Their voice was wistful. They weren't even scowling anymore.

Without meaning to, all five of them had stopped walking. They stood in a circle, each looking uncomfortable and sad. Riley wished she could think of something to say. This was a Rule #2 moment, a time for encouraging others. That's what an alpha would do.

But how was she supposed to encourage others when she felt like this? Like sadness was a pair of iron shoes strapped to her feet. All she could manage was a soft "Me, too."

Several yards away, Bethany's head was just visible

above the tall grass, bobbing along like a ship on the waves.

"Maybe Aracely was right all along and we're all a year younger than we thought," Riley suggested. "Maybe we've got another year and it's all the most ridiculous mistake there ever was."

"My uncles do really suck at math," Lydia agreed.

"My parents had five kids," Aracely chimed in. "I would absolutely believe they lost track of one."

"My parents are very good at math," Kenver said thoughtfully. "But I guess I could buy an elaborate switched-at-birth fiasco."

"My dad always says I'm actually a faerie child who wandered in from the woods one day," Dhonielle offered with a small smile.

"My moms mix us up all the time. Sometimes with the cats. And they're all named after trees!" Riley finished.

Lydia actually snorted at that, then slapped one hand across her mouth in shock. For a second, she stared straight ahead, avoiding looking at any of them, then she began to laugh.

And then they were all laughing. In spite of the growing heat and the bug bites, in spite of the fact that they were all in trouble, it felt good to laugh. Maybe they weren't real wolves, maybe Riley wasn't an alpha, but maybe, just maybe, it was going to be okay.

16

THE PACK THAT DREAMS TOGETHER SCREAMS TOGETHER

"Here we are!" Bethany said brightly. "Welcome to the Stone Pool."

They'd come into a valley where a pool of bright blue water glittered in the sunlight. It was shaped like a teardrop and surrounded by slabs of gray stone just like the ones that made up the paths in the main village. Wildflowers scattered around the fringes, adding splashes of pale purple and dark yellow to the scene.

"I have a bad feeling we aren't here to go swimming." Aracely stared longingly at the pool.

Riley couldn't blame her. After their long, sweaty walk through the grass, the idea of jumping into that crystal-clear pool was almost too tempting.

A few feet from the edge of the water, Bethany stooped and plucked a cloudy moonstone from within a patch of dark green grass. Then, closing her eyes, she rubbed her thumb over its surface in a slow, deliberate circle.

There was a soft hissing sound and a ring of cloudy light appeared before their eyes. It spun around the pool like mist, then dissipated into thin air.

"Why does the pool have its own ward?" Riley asked. "Isn't there already a ward around Clawroot?"

"Not to mention all of Wax & Wayne?" Kenver added.

"Must be something important," Lydia said thoughtfully.

Bethany dropped the moonstone back into the grass and gestured for them to follow. "Good questions, and you're right, Lydia. The Stone Pool is one of our magic sites, so even though Wax & Wayne and Clawroot are protected, there are some places we need to keep extra safe."

"From who?" Riley asked.

"Or what?" Dhonielle added.

"Exactly," Bethany answered. "We do our best to make sure all the wolves know what they need to, but sometimes people forget, or they might stumble into something they shouldn't. Accidents happen. Wards help us make sure they happen less frequently."

"What's so special about this place?" Aracely asked.

"This is where we cleanse and charge our stones to use in lithomancy. Take a look."

Riley stepped up to the edge and peered into the clear

blue water. Sunlight speared the surface at an angle, creating shafts of light that dove down, down, down. Little fish darted back and forth, making flashes of silver and brown. Riley wasn't sure what she was supposed to be looking at until something glimmered all the way at the bottom of the pool.

Lined up in neat rows that stretched from one side to the other were stones. Most were the recognizable tan of the sandstone that was everywhere in Kansas, but some were slabs of gray slate, chunks of shiny black basalt, even a few eggs of moonstone and something pink.

"Every stone we use for lithomancy has to be prepared properly," Bethany explained, sounding very much like one of their Tenderfoot Camp teachers. "They charge here, in the sun and the moon and the wild energy of our woods, and when they're ready, we take them back to the village to be enspelled."

Riley eyed the water skeptically. She had a sudden sinking feeling that she knew exactly what their punishment was going to be.

"Um, Miss Bethany, do you expect us to dive all the way down there and haul rocks back to the surface?" Riley asked.

"Of course not!" Bethany answered, smiling a little too widely. "I expect you to pick up those stones over there and help me get them to the Litho House."

She pointed to a spot where dozens of stones were so

neatly stacked, Riley had taken them for a low wall. Every stone looked big. And heavy.

"Cool!" Aracely raced toward the rocks, while the rest of them gawked after her.

"There is definitely something wrong with her," Lydia muttered.

Riley looked up in surprise. Lydia was close enough that their elbows brushed, and Riley could smell the rosemary soap she'd used to wash her face this morning, could see the spot on Lydia's cheek that was almost a dimple. All of a sudden, all Riley could think about was how pretty Lydia was and how thinking that made her feel fluttery and strange.

"Um, yep, uh, yeah," Riley answered, unsure why she was having so much trouble making words.

Her cheeks burned as Lydia bent to inspect the rocks with Aracely.

"How are we supposed to lift those?" Dhonielle was asking, hands twisted nervously in front of her.

"Like this," Aracely said before Bethany could answer.

Aracely reached out and pressed one hand flat against a large piece of sandstone. Closing her eyes, she mouthed the word *lift*. Words weren't strictly necessary in wolf magic, but it didn't hurt to say the thing you were imagining, especially if it was the first time.

Aracely opened her eyes again and slowly drew her arm up. The stone rose with her hand as though it were a balloon filled with helium and only her hand was keeping it from floating into the sky.

"Exactly," Bethany said with approval. "All right, everyone pick a stone. We have a lot of hauling to get through and I'd like to finish before lunch."

"I don't think I can do that." Dhonielle eyed a stone skeptically.

"Of course you can. I bet you already know how to do it. You just have to imagine the rock is a part of you instead of the ground, you know? Imagine that it's like an extra hand or something. Like this." Aracely demonstrated once more, showing Dhonielle exactly how to place her hand and how to draw it up slowly. "Now you try."

One by one, they pressed their palms against a stone and did exactly as Aracely had done. Riley chose a piece of granite with a red vein running through the middle that reminded her of Blood Creek. As she laid her hand against the cool stone, she felt the subtle vibration within. A similar vibration echoed in her chest. She closed her eyes and visualized the stone rising as though weightless.

When she opened her eyes again, the stone hovered a few feet off the ground. Though it was rough to the touch, she felt like she could bounce it like a ball if she tried. Which she did not.

"Everyone ready?" Bethany surveyed their handiwork, then nodded in satisfaction. "All right, let's go. You have a lot of stones to move."

The trek between the pool and the Litho House was easy enough at first. Each time they arrived at the Litho House, Aaron Walsey met them at the door with an apron around his waist and a chuckle. "Strong work, strong work!" he shouted, directing them to place the stones on tables or shelves or stack them neatly in corners. Then he'd add, "Next time you see these stones, they'll be keeping pests away from our tomatoes!" or "Next time you see these stones, they'll be lighting the way through the woods!" or "Next time you see these stones, well, you won't 'cause they'll be buried along the ward line!"

As they traveled back and forth, they all found ways to pass the time. Riley kicked off a game of twenty questions, Dhonielle led them in a round of their favorite camp songs, Lydia told stories of her uncles' greatest bakery disasters, and Kenver won round after round of the memory game while Aracely challenged herself to see how many stones she could carry at once. The answer was always three, but that didn't stop her from trying to add a fourth.

By the afternoon, they were covered in sweat, tiny cuts on their arms and cheeks from razor-sharp grasses, and a dozen new bug bites, but they were still laughing and smiling. They'd learned how to work together and somehow that made the work feel less like work.

After they'd moved the last of the stones, Bethany gave

them permission to swim for a few minutes and cool off. The words were barely out of her mouth before Aracely was running and tucking into a perfect cannonball that made a massive splash.

"Aracely! Don't you get my hair wet!" Dhonielle raised a finger in warning, but she was smiling, too.

They swam long enough for their fingers to get wrinkled. When it was time to go, they climbed out of the pool and woefully eyed the way back to Clawroot. There was nothing quite as uncomfortable as walking a long distance in wet clothing.

Kenver placed their hands flat against their chest, one on top of the other. They stayed that way for a minute before Riley realized what was happening. Little by little, Kenver's clothing was going from wet to dry. The changes were subtle at first, then the soaked fabric gradually unstuck itself from their skin. The drying effect moved down shoulders to ankles until there was no water left.

"Um, teach me that one, please," Aracely said. "That was alchemy, right?"

Alchemy, or transformational magic, was the practice of changing one thing into another. The only catch was that the two things had to be related. Sticks or hedge apples could be transformed into paper, for example, or silver could be reshaped and turned into bronze, but while a lollipop could become a Popsicle or a bit of cotton candy, it couldn't become a scarf or a T-shirt.

Riley knew that from personal experimentation.

Alchemical magic was the part of the magical triad that allowed their bodies to shift between human and wolf. The ability to change was an essential part of who they were.

"Liquid to gas," Dhonielle said, understanding exactly what Kenver had achieved. "I don't think that would have occurred to me!"

"Alchemy just sort of makes sense to me," Kenver admitted shyly. "Besides, I really hate not being in control of my body. I mean, the parts I can control. Like being wet or dirty or—"

Kenver stopped, as though they hadn't meant to share even that much.

"Alchemy feels really right to me," they added. "Everything is always changing a little bit anyway. Alchemy just helps it along."

"Do me!" Aracely bounced up to Kenver and held her arms out to either side.

Tentatively, Kenver laid their hands against Aracely's shoulders. Aracely giggled immediately, then said, "Sorry, sorry, sorry. I'm ticklish. But I can do this." She took a deep breath and closed her eyes while Kenver worked.

Kenver made it look so easy. Their hands drew the water from the cloth and released it into the air as though summoning the individual molecules. If only there were a way to do that with their wolves.

The thought stopped Riley in her tracks.

"Ms. Books, what is the Summoning Rite?" she asked.

Surprise flashed across Bethany's features for a split second before her signature smile reappeared. "Is that what you were poking around for last night?"

Riley nodded as the others shifted closer to listen.

"Well, it's a special ceremony that is sometimes used to try and lure a wolf out," Bethany explained. "It's not something we use frequently, but every so often, when a wolf experiences something traumatic, their magic can get blocked and they need a little help finding it again."

That made Riley think of Auntie Fang, who had gone away to war in her teens and come back without her wolf. Riley had been too young to know the details, but somewhere along the way, Auntie Fang had found her magic again and taken up her post at the forge. Now she was mostly a hermit, turning silver into wolf cuffs from day to day. She wasn't Riley's blood aunt. In fact, Riley wasn't sure if she was any pup's actual aunt, but she was everyone's auntie.

"Is . . . did Auntie Fang have a Summoning Rite?" Riley asked.

Bethany nodded without elaborating. "We sometimes use them when people want to leave the pack, too. When they don't want the wolf inside them anymore."

Riley couldn't imagine not wanting her wolf, though

she knew some people made that choice. That was the gift First Wolf had given to every wolf in the world when she cast her spell: the ability to choose.

"Do you think it would work on us?" Riley asked.

Bethany adjusted her glasses and made a small clucking noise with her tongue. "It is a possibility," she admitted with extreme reluctance.

"But?" Riley pressed.

"But we have only ever used it on adults." She paused before adding, "It's tremendously painful. We don't want to put any of you through it if we can help it, so we're looking for other options."

"Because we're so young?" Riley asked.

"That, and because you're not—" Bethany stopped herself.

Not real wolves, the voice in Riley's head added in a taunting whisper.

"Because you haven't transformed even once." Bethany smiled apologetically. "We simply don't know what it would do to you."

"Oh" was all Riley could say. Disappointment sat heavy in her throat.

Soon they were on their way back to the village. By the time dinner was done and they'd returned to the cabin for the night, they were practically asleep on their feet. No one uttered a complaint when the lights automatically snapped off at nine. All five pups fell into a deep sleep of tangled dreams that twisted into darker and darker corners.

Riley was running through the woods. The light of the full moon splintered between the canopy of oak and maple leaves, painting sycamore trunks in ghostly white. She was afraid, but of what?

Something behind her.

Something was following her, chasing her, tracking her.

She ran harder, pumping her arms and legs as fast as they would go. All she knew was that she had to hurry, to get somewhere before he did. To find the others, to find the stone and . . .

A wolf call pierced the night and Riley gasped. It wasn't an ordinary call, but a warning. A call like that meant one thing: danger!

Riley kept running. She wanted to call out for help but was afraid of who, or what, would hear her.

She ran and ran until finally, just ahead, she saw light. She made directly for it.

Cold sweat streaked down her back and she could hear whatever it was crashing through the woods behind her. She could smell it closing in and it smelled like old, wet leaves and electricity.

She ran harder.

She burst out of the woods and into a moon-bright

clearing. In the center of it was a tall stone. Its granite surface glittered darkly.

"Grace." A name whispered on the breeze. Her name. "Grace."

Riley shook her head in confusion. She was Riley, she knew that. But she was also Grace.

Suddenly, four other figures stepped out of the woods. Four faces that Grace knew. They stood in a perfect ring around the stone. Their eyes were wide with fear.

"He's coming."

Something crashed directly behind Riley and a growl rumbled in her ear.

"Now!" Grace shouted. "It has to be n—"

Riley woke up suddenly, bolting upright and breathing hard. Moonlight streamed through the window, making swirling leaf patterns against the floor. The sounds of harsh breathing came from every side of the room, from every bed.

Riley glanced around.

Four faces stared back at her in the dark.

Whatever had just happened, it had happened to all of them.

We trapped him in a prison of stone because it was the only thing strong enough to hold him. We hid that stone inside a ringward so that no one would ever find him. No one could ever release him.

But if this diary has found you, if you are reading this, then something has gone wrong. The ward has withered. The stone has cracked. Whatever it is, he has escaped.

And he will come for you.

17

THE CABIN
AT THE END OF THE ROW

"That was real, right?" Aracely asked. "We all had that dream?"

They huddled in Riley's bed, feet and shoulders pressed together with a pile of Aracely's stuffed animals between them. It turned out one of Aracely's bags had been filled with nothing but stuffed animals. There were cats and bears and lots of dinosaurs. Riley had never really cared about stuffed animals, but right now, she was very glad to have them.

"It was real," Riley assured her.

"Why did it happen?" Lydia held a stuffed stegosaurus in her lap. It was neon green with hot-pink plates down its back.

Riley didn't have an answer, but this felt important. It felt like whatever had happened to keep them from transforming during the Full Moon Rite was also connecting their dreams. She just didn't know yet if it was a good sign or a bad one.

"We should tell Aunt CeCe," Dhonielle suggested, looking to Riley for confirmation. "Whatever is happening to us is still happening. We need to tell an adult."

Riley was only a little surprised to find she didn't disagree. This definitely seemed like inform-an-adult territory. In fact, it seemed like Rule #4 territory. Another time to do the tough stuff.

"What about the Summoning Rite?" Riley asked.

"What does that have to do with the dream?" Kenver asked.

"Nothing," Riley admitted. "But it's something to try."

Dhonielle squeezed the stuffed wolf in her arms. "Bethany Books said they've never tried it on kids. She said it would hurt."

Riley nodded. "I know, but I'd rather try something than wait around to see what's next."

"I agree," Lydia said.

"Me, too," added Kenver.

Riley turned to Aracely, who only nodded, then back to Dhonielle.

"Okay," Dhonielle said after a long pause.

"Okay," Riley repeated. "First thing in the morning, then, we'll find my mom, tell her about the dream, and ask her about the Summoning Rite."

Everyone agreed and reluctantly returned to their

own beds. Eventually Riley fell into a fitful sleep, her dreams haunted by shadowy figures and strange crashing noises, but whatever had happened in the middle of the night, it didn't happen again.

Riley awoke, bleary-eyed and anxious and very clearly the last one up. Again. Kenver popped their head in from the front room. "Something's happening outside," they said.

Riley was out of bed in an instant and dressed a second later. She only barely convinced herself to go brush her teeth before rushing out the door. Just like yesterday, she found the others waiting for her on the cabin porch. But unlike yesterday, Clawroot was buzzing with activity. It was early and the sun was slicing through the trees at a steep angle, but there were more wolves and people around than they'd seen since they'd arrived.

The five of them raced off the porch, following the noise and activity all the way to the center of Clawroot. Everyone was gathering on the green in front of the Hall of Ancestors where Mama C was shouting orders.

"Murphy! Hudson! Taylor!" she called, glancing down at a notebook. "Are you all here?"

Three voices piped up in response, "Here!"

"I want you in the Eastern Sweep from the creek to the property line. Stay together. I don't want anyone caught out there alone!"

Murphy, Hudson, and Taylor moved out of the crowd.

Behind them, the members of their primes followed. Once they were on the edge of the green, they began to transform. Their bodies shimmered and shifted, their noses stretching into muzzles, their hands and feet into powerful paws, their skin feathering with soft fur. Then the three prime packs raced off, shooting out of the clearing like bolts of light.

Mama C called more names, handing out assignments as swiftly as new wolves arrived. She looked calm and in command of the situation. The perfect pack alpha.

"Something bad happened," Dhonielle muttered at Riley's side.

Riley nodded absently as she studied the crowd. Everyone looked upset, worried, or flat-out angry. They spoke in low murmurs, but for the most part they watched Mama C, waiting for her to direct them.

The greater pack routinely patrolled all of Wax & Wayne, but Riley had never heard of them doing an organized search like this. Something bad had definitely happened.

"Riley!" The call came from behind and the five of them spun at the sound.

"Darcy!" Riley raced to meet her sister.

"I'm so sorry I wasn't there," Darcy said, wrapping Riley in a huge hug. She smelled like the woods and like wolves. "Are you okay? I mean, I know you're okay, but are you okay?"

"I'm fine, I promise," Riley said as Darcy released her and took a small step back.

"Hey," she said. "It's okay if you're not, you know?"

Darcy always, always knew when Riley was putting on a brave face.

Riley's lips quivered, but she smiled. "I know," she said.

A suspicious frown bent Darcy's lips and she tugged Riley closer as Mama C issued more orders and wolves darted into the woods. "Listen to me. What's happening to you right now sucks. It's hard to feel like you can't control parts of your body. But the transformation isn't what makes you a wolf. You do that with or without magic."

"I'd rather do it with magic," Riley said.

"Honestly, same, but the great thing about being a wolf is that we get to choose it. Even when we don't."

That didn't make any sense to Riley, but she shrugged anyway.

"Hey, coz. How about you? You doing okay?" Darcy opened her arms and folded Dhonielle into another hug.

Instead of speaking, Dhonielle just nodded against Darcy, biting her lip to keep from crying.

"What are you doing here? I thought you were out with Milo and the new wolves?" Riley asked.

Darcy and her prime were supposed to stay with the newly transformed pups until they were ready to return. Darcy should be with Milo. Not here. Not human.

"I was. Until . . ." Darcy looked toward the crowd.

"What's going on?" Riley asked.

"You haven't heard?" Darcy seemed surprised.

Riley shook her head and tried to ignore the slithering voice in her head that whispered, *They didn't wake you because you're not a real wolf.*

"They called us all in because of . . ." She hesitated before continuing. "Because of what happened to Luke a few nights ago, and now Paislee."

"What do you mean? What happened to them?" Riley asked.

"Were there hunters out there?" Dhonielle asked.

"Did they get caught?" Aracely added.

"Are they hurt?" Riley was feeling worse by the second.

"Slow down," Darcy soothed, opening her mouth to say more, but just then Mama C shouted, "Westfall!" And Darcy's eyes jumped to find the alpha of her prime, Evan Westfall, as he answered, "Here!"

"That's us. I have to go," she said apologetically. "They're . . . well, I won't say they're okay, exactly. Actually, you might want to go talk to them yourself."

"*Talk* to them?" Riley asked, horror flickering in her throat. There was no way they should be able to talk to Luke Shacklett or Paislee Scott right now. Because Luke and Paislee were wolves.

But Darcy nodded sadly. "They're in cabin six."

She pointed to the last cabin in the row. Where Ms. Montgomery had taken Mama C on their first day in

Clawroot and where Riley had seen Mama C and Bethany arguing in the middle of the night.

Before she left, Darcy hugged Riley one more time. In spite of being small, she was strong, and her hugs always made Riley feel safe. She squeezed Darcy back just as tightly, wishing they'd had more than a few minutes to talk.

The rest of the wolves were too wrapped up in organizing their search to notice the five of them. They cut across the lawn and counted down the cabins until they reached number six.

Riley tentatively knocked at the door.

No one answered, so Riley knocked a little harder.

"Maybe we should come back later?" Dhonielle suggested.

Riley leaned her ear against the door and listened. Everything was perfectly quiet. She pulled back and only hesitated a second before twisting the knob and pushing the door open a few inches.

"Hello?" she called.

Again there was no answer. The cabin felt empty, but the lights were on in the bedroom.

Riley pushed the door open a little wider and stepped inside.

"I don't think we should be doing this. If something is really wrong with them, this could be dangerous," Dhonielle whispered, but Riley kept going.

Darcy wouldn't have sent them into danger. But even as she thought it, she felt the hairs prickling on the nape of her neck.

Something was wrong.

Inside, the cabin was an exact replica of the one they were staying in, right down to the colors in the carpets. It even kind of smelled the same: like pine and the clean soapy scent of fresh sheets.

And sweat.

Riley wrinkled her nose. "Luke? Paislee?"

"Hello?" Luke's weak voice called from the bedroom. "We're in here."

They found him in one of the beds with pillows piled behind him to prop him up. He looked pale and exhausted, with dark purple rings beneath his eyes. On the other side of the room, Paislee was in another bed, her eyes tightly shut.

"Riley?" Luke asked, blinking at them. "Lydia? Oh. Hi."

He shrank back against the pillows and tugged at the covers. He looked uncharacteristically small and unsure of himself. And sick.

"Are—are you okay?" Riley asked. Then, realizing that she could see he was definitely *not* okay, she added, "What happened to you? Is Paislee . . . is she . . . ?"

"Asleep," Luke said. "Dr. Khorram gave her something to help keep her calm."

Kenver offered him a cup of water from the bedside

table. He took it and sipped, but even that seemed to take more energy than he had.

"What happened to you? Why aren't you in the South Wood with the others?" Riley asked.

Luke stared at the wall across the room. The corners of his lips quivered, and his eyes grew glassy with unshed tears. Whatever it was he wanted to say, it was something truly terrible.

Riley held her breath.

"I'm not a wolf anymore," Luke said at last. Big tears rolled down his sallow cheeks and he choked out a sob before adding, "My wolf is gone!"

18

SOMETHING IN THE WOODS

"What do you mean?" Riley asked. "How can your wolf be gone?"

Again Luke's eyes welled up, but this time, he looked more afraid than anything else. His voice was small when he answered, "It happened on the very first night. I'd only been a wolf for a few hours. Everything is still sort of blurry. I remember feeling like something was calling me away from the pack. I remember being alone and then I could just *feel* something coming so I ran." He shook his head. "I never should have stopped running."

Luke shivered and seemed to fade into the memory.

He'd been here the whole time they had, and no one had told them.

"Luke?" Riley kept her voice soft. "What happened then?"

"It was just . . . there."

"What was?" Riley asked, horror inching up her throat.

"The forest? A tornado? I don't really know. It sounded

like a storm was coming in, but there was no rain. Just the smell of wet leaves and then this growl."

Riley turned to Lydia. They wore matching expressions of surprise.

More tears splashed down Luke's cheeks. "It seemed like it was everywhere. All around me. And then—"

Riley reached out and took Luke's hand. His skin was hot, and his eyes flashed immediately to hers.

"I could feel its magic. It was cold like I'd inhaled fog and then it hurt. It hurt so much." He shuddered. "And then it was gone. Over. Bethany Books was there, helping me up. She kept telling me not to panic and that I was fine. I was going to be fine. I didn't really know what she was talking about at first. But then . . . I felt it. Or I guess I *didn't* feel it."

Luke drifted into silence. His eyes stared straight ahead while the tears dried on his cheeks. It seemed like he'd forgotten they were in the room with him.

Riley looked over to where Paislee was still fast asleep. Her skin was pale and shiny with sweat and she moaned every once in a while.

"Did it happen to Paislee, too?" she asked.

Luke nodded sadly. "Last night."

Riley couldn't imagine what this must feel like, and for a second, she was glad she hadn't become a wolf with the others. At least her wolf was still somewhere inside her.

The thought made her feel guilty and uncomfortable.

"Are you sure that it's gone?" Riley asked.

Suddenly, Luke was sitting up, his eyes ablaze with anger.

"I'm not! A wolf! Anymore!" Luke shouted.

Riley felt her cheeks warming with embarrassment and hurt, but Lydia crossed her arms and scowled at Luke.

"Hey! Just because you're mad doesn't mean you get to be mad at Riley," Lydia snapped. "You're not the only one here who isn't a wolf, you know. So stop acting like it."

Riley felt her mouth drop open. And then the warmth in her cheeks burned even hotter. Lydia Edgerton was defending her.

Luke glared at Lydia for a minute, but his anger was fading fast. He blew out a breath and turned back to Riley.

"I'm sorry, Riley," he said. "I'm not mad at you, I'm just . . ."

He didn't finish his sentence, but Riley thought she understood a little of how he was feeling. It must be different to have been a wolf and then have it taken away as opposed to never turning into one in the first place.

"It's okay," she said.

He smiled like he was still sorry and maybe a little embarrassed that he had lashed out.

Kenver spoke up for the first time. "Do they know what it was?"

"Great Leader Callahan thinks I must have run into some sort of hunters' snare. The same kind that got your mom, Dhonielle. Bethany Books thought it could also be a witches' lure. But no one has ever heard of a witches' lure taking this much magic from anyone." He sighed. "Not to mention that the wards haven't been broken so the chances of someone running around out there setting traps is, like, impossible or something."

This must have been what Mama C meant when she told Riley there was something in the woods. This was why she wanted them to stay in Clawroot. It was also why she was sending the rest of the pack into the woods right now. The wolves who were in their first transformation, wolves like Milo, couldn't turn back into humans without interrupting their magic. It was up to the rest of the pack to protect them. To search for whatever was doing this.

"They'll figure it out," Riley said, trying to sound more confident than she felt.

"And then they'll fix you," Aracely sang. "I mean, right?"

Dhonielle shrugged softly. "They haven't fixed us."

Luke collapsed back against his pillows. There was a fresh sheen of sweat across his brow and his eyes looked heavy.

"We should let you rest," Lydia said.

"We're just three cabins down that way if you need anything," Kenver said helpfully.

Luke nodded weakly, giving them a little wave as they left.

Outside, they spotted the last of the wolves running into the woods. Mama C was in the lead, her dark brown coat and silver muzzle flashing in the sunlight. As soon as they'd passed, Clawroot was silent. Even though they knew better, it felt as if they were all alone.

"We're thinking the same thing, right?" Kenver asked as the five of them headed toward a long-overdue breakfast. "There's something out there in the woods that isn't a witch or a hunter?"

"But what else is there?" Aracely asked.

Riley only shook her head. Mama C and Bethany Books were smart. If they thought it could be a hunter or a witch, then they must have good reasons. Right?

"He heard a growl, too," Lydia reminded them. "And we heard another last night in the dream. That can't be a coincidence. What could be doing this?"

The nightmare flashed through Riley's mind in vivid colors. There were too many similarities to ignore. From being chased through the woods to the smell of wet leaves to the growl. But that wasn't the thing that was sending shivers skittering down Riley's backbone.

There was only one thing she'd ever heard of that could steal a person's wolf away. And it was something they'd read about just last night.

She paused and looked at the others before whispering, "The Devouring Wolf."

19

TECHNICALLY DEAD AND ALIVE

That stopped them in their tracks.

"The Devourer?" Kenver clarified. "Who stole the wolves of his prime pack so that he could become more powerful than any other living wolf?"

Dhonielle whimpered.

"But he's . . . not . . . real?" Aracely asked.

"I know," Riley said, though part of her wasn't entirely sure. "But I can't quit thinking about the story Dhonielle found in the archive. About there being five tenderfoot pups who didn't transform when he rose up, and now this. I just think even if the Devourer himself wasn't real, maybe there's a little bit of truth to the stories."

"What does that mean?" Aracely frowned in confusion.

"She means that the magic could be real," Kenver explained. "And obviously *is* if people are having their wolves stolen away."

"Okay, but the story is definitely *not* real, right?" Aracely asked. "The Devourer died, and therefore we aren't talking about the actual Devourer, right?'

"Well," Dhonielle started, then stopped, shrinking back as four heads turned toward her. "Maybe?"

"What does that mean?" Riley pressed.

Dhonielle squeezed herself a little harder. "It's just that in the story, they never actually say that he died. They say he was too powerful to kill."

Lydia gasped. "That's right! The story ends when he's trapped inside a stone. Not killed. Trapped."

"What?!" Aracely's voice jumped about a thousand decibels. "You mean if—and this is the biggest *if* in the history of ifs—but *if* the story is real, then he's been *alive* inside a rock all this time?!"

"Not technically?" Dhonielle looked like she wanted to melt into the ground beneath her feet.

"How can someone be not technically alive *or* dead?" Aracely demanded. "You have to be one or the other!"

"You don't have to shout," Lydia said, crossing her arms smoothly over her chest.

"Yeah, but—" Aracely snapped her mouth shut and nodded. "Okay, okay, okay. Sorry, Dhonielle."

Dhonielle blinked owlishly, then said, "Magic."

"Huh?" Aracely and Lydia said in unison.

"That's how he could be not technically alive or dead: magic. Like the story says, they encased him in a stone and a curse and then they put him where he would be forgotten."

Riley's mouth dropped open. "They encased him in stone."

Lydia sucked in a breath, her brown eyes widening.

"Like the one in our dream?" Aracely asked, voice threatening to climb again.

Dhonielle shrugged. "I guess. It would have to be a pretty big one to trap him."

The stone from their dream had been large. Wide enough that it would take all five of them to stretch their arms around it; tall enough that Riley wouldn't be able to reach the top without a boost.

All at once, Riley felt the pieces of the puzzle falling into place—the five of them were sharing dreams and mysterious growls. Then Luke's and Paislee's wolves had been ripped away, and the stone from their dream wasn't just any stone, it was clearly magical and very important.

"It's the Devouring Wolf. It has to be," Riley said. Then another thought landed, this one even more horrifying. "And Mama C just sent all the wolves out to look for him!"

Before she knew it, she was running. Racing toward the woods. She felt the moment her cuff shivered as she passed the ward of Clawroot, but she did not stop. Her mom had given her a task, to come tell her if she noticed anything strange, and this was more than strange. It was dangerous. She had to tell her.

Tree limbs bobbed above like jagged teeth while the underbrush curved below, transforming the woods into a deadly grin. The air was alive with birdcalls and the incessant buzzing of summer bugs. Riley ran and ran. The only thought in her mind was to warn her mom.

Every wolf in Wax & Wayne was in danger and they didn't even know it.

But where were they? Riley's mind caught up with her body. She skidded to a stop.

Something crashed into her from behind, sending her flying onto her stomach with an "Oof!"

Panic swept through Riley. The Devouring Wolf had found her. He had her pinned. His fur tickled her cheek and his hot breath wafted against her ear. Then—

"Sorry, sorry, sorry!" Aracely scrambled off of Riley, collecting leaves and sticks in her curls.

Riley rolled onto her back, head spinning.

Lydia appeared standing over her, a pinch of worry on her pretty face. She offered a hand, helping Riley onto her feet once more. Riley rubbed at a bruise forming on her hip as the other two came rushing up.

"You run too fast," Dhonielle complained.

"You run too slow," Aracely snapped back.

"You both run just fine," Lydia soothed, always the peacemaker.

"We have to warn them," Riley said, turning to search the woods.

"I have an idea," Kenver said, a small smile on their lips. Then they tipped their head back and began to howl. The thin note was laced with wolf magic and bore a single message: *Come.*

Riley added her call to theirs and soon all five of them were howling together, asking the wolves to come find them.

It worked faster than any of them expected. When they saw shapes gliding through the underbrush, they stopped howling and waited. Riley held her breath, trying to practice what she was going to say in her head, and when she saw her mom's silver muzzle nose through green bushes, she sighed in relief.

But her relief was short-lived. The wolf in front of her shimmered and shivered as the transformation began. Her deep brown fur smoothed away, her ears slimmed down against her head, and her body rolled upright into the form of Mama C. And she was glowering at Riley.

"What do you think you're doing here?" her mom demanded.

All the courage Riley had felt as she raced into the woods shrank under the pressing weight of Mama C's gaze. "Um," she began.

"Any of you." Mama C shared her displeasure with the other four, drawing an audible gulp from Dhonielle.

"We have something important to tell you," Riley said, hating that her voice already sounded whiney and plaintive. Why did that always happen when she was talking to adults?

"And it couldn't wait?" Mama C crossed her arms. Even the rest of the wolves seemed to be keeping their distance. Riley didn't recognize them immediately, which was odd. Mama C always ran with her prime, but there was no sign of Aunt Alexis or Crow, Kate, or Nic.

"Well?" Mama C snapped, obliterating all curiosity from Riley's mind.

"The Devouring Wolf!" Riley blurted out.

Her mom's expression darkened. Her eyes narrowed dangerously and in an instant she became Great Callahan.

"Riley Callahan, you have endangered everyone here by leading them out of Clawroot like this." Great Callahan planted her hands on her hips, disappointment dripping from every word. "This is irresponsible and reckless and not the kind of behavior I expect of you."

"I'm sorry, but it's true. It has to be," Riley continued. She wished she could sound more authoritative and less like a kid. Instead she tried to mirror the way her mom stood with hands on hips, shoulders back, and chin high. "I can explain—"

"I'm not interested in you doing anything except going back." Her mom looked scarier now, her eyes narrowed and gleaming. "You told me I could trust you, but here you are, crying wolf and putting everyone in needless danger. This is no way for a young pup to behave."

Riley heard the shuffle of feet behind her and knew it was Dhonielle. Just like she knew the eyes of Kenver, Aracely, and Lydia were on her right now. Watching as her mom dressed her down in front of everyone.

"I want you all to return to Clawroot *now*."

Riley swallowed her embarrassment and tried one more time. "I know how it sounds, but the Devouring Wolf was the only one who could steal a person's wolf away. He's real and we think he's out here!"

"Oh, do you?" Great Callahan's voice was knife-sharp. "So not only is the story true, but he's here. Right now. In these very woods?"

"Mom, I—"

"No! Stop right there, Riley. This is wolf business. You need to leave it to the wolves." Great Callahan's body shimmered as the transformation began. "I am very disappointed in you right now. Go home."

Riley felt the tears straining in her throat. Her feet were glued to the ground, holding her body in place as though movement would somehow make this feel even worse. But she wasn't sure anything could feel worse than watching her mom dive toward the forest floor and race away with the rest of the wolves.

The rest of the real wolves.

Leaving Riley and the others behind.

20

DECISIONS WITHOUT ADULTS

Riley felt like a slug that had been covered in salt and left to writhe on the concrete. Her insides were all shriveled and tight, her skin was clammy, and she was pretty sure her voice had slunk out of her throat and deposited itself all the way down in her toes, never to be heard again.

She had never been so thoroughly reprimanded by Mama C. Especially not in front of so many people.

She suddenly ached for Mama N to appear, to wrap her up in a big hug and tell her it was just a misunderstanding. Mama C wasn't *actually* that mad at her.

But Mama C had never looked at her with such keen disapproval before. Had never been so clear that Riley was not a wolf.

Not a real *wolf.* The words slithered through her thoughts as a worm through a rotten apple.

None of this would be happening if she'd transformed when she was supposed to. Mama C wouldn't be so disappointed in her daughter if she'd become a wolf with the others.

And there was absolutely nothing Riley could do to fix that. To prove to Mama C that she was capable of being a real wolf.

Except maybe there was.

"The Summoning Rite!" They were the first words Riley had uttered the whole way back to Clawroot, and Dhonielle yelped in surprise.

"What are you shouting about?" Dhonielle asked, one hand pressed against her heart.

"I don't think we're going to convince your mom to do that right now." Lydia tipped her head to the side and studied Riley closely. "Oh, you don't want to ask permission."

"I don't. The description of the rite was straightforward. All we have to do is follow the instructions. The only problem is that we have to find the heart of wolves, whatever that is."

Kenver stepped forward. "Um, I know what that is. More importantly, though, I know where it is."

"What? How?" Riley asked in delighted surprise.

"I told you, I like magic. The Heart of Wolves exists at the nexus of the three forms of wolf magic—it's a cave deep in the earth, with a heart of stone, where howls are concentrated and contained. And it's right here in Claw-root."

"Caves! I'm in," Aracely announced.

"But." Dhonielle chewed on her bottom lip. "Bethany Books said it would hurt, remember?"

"You don't have to go first," Riley assured her. "We'll try it on one of us, and if it doesn't work, then you don't have to do it at all."

"I'll go first." Lydia raised a hand.

"Really? That's so brave," Aracely said appreciatively.

Riley almost bit her tongue.

Once again, Lydia had made herself the most important person in the group. Riley struggled to swallow the ugly feelings climbing up from her belly, but it was challenging. This had been *her* plan!

"I can do it," Riley said, doing her best not to choke on her irritation. "I'm not afraid."

"I know, but someone has to actually do the rite," Lydia said with a small smile. "Shouldn't that be you?"

Riley thought about that for a minute. It was true that someone had to lead the rite. Someone had to stay alert and level-headed while the magic worked. Even though this felt like a moment for Rule #4, Riley realized leaders couldn't always be the ones doing the tough stuff. Sometimes they had to delegate the tough stuff. That was Rule #5: *Trust your pack.*

"Okay," Riley said decisively. "We have a plan."

They made a quick stop at cabin three for Lydia's journal, then Kenver led them down a trail that dipped into the woods and turned north. This definitely wasn't what Mama C had meant when she'd said "Go home," but technically, they were still inside the Clawroot ward, so they weren't breaking any rules.

"It's really not a very complicated rite," Lydia said, walking at Riley's side with the journal open so Riley could see. "The person whose wolf is being called sits in the center, and the remaining wolves, ideally those in their prime, call to the wolf inside."

"Sounds easy enough," Riley said even though she was starting to feel nervous. Wolf magic wasn't like witch magic or hunter magic. It didn't require special ingredients or charms. It came from inside. It was instinct and intention, which meant they had what they needed to perform this rite. But it also meant there would be nothing to protect them if it went wrong.

The air chilled as Kenver led them to a hill that was sheared flat on one side. Kenver knelt and pressed one hand to a stone buried in the ground. After a second, the hillside rippled and a cave opened wide like a mouth ready to swallow them up.

"Is this it?" Riley asked.

"The Heart of Wolves," Kenver answered reverently.

Riley glanced at Lydia. "You're sure you want to do this?"

"I'm sure," Lydia answered.

"Ready?" Kenver asked. They were standing at the mouth of the cave. Next to them, Aracely held a litho-charm in her hands. It glowed softly.

"I hate the dark," Dhonielle muttered.

Lydia sucked in a breath. Riley stepped up next to her, then together they said, "Ready," and stepped inside.

21

THE SUMMONING RITE

L ong, winding tunnels led deep underground, twisting through the darkness until Riley had thoroughly
lost her sense of direction.

They came to a stop inside a room shaped like a sphere.
The ceiling curved above them like a stone sky, while the
floor dipped away at their feet. A ledge just wide enough
for a single person to walk comfortably encircled the
room. Wolflight shone softly along the walls, giving the
pale sandstone a warm glow. In addition to the tunnel
they'd arrived through, three others opened around the
room at equal intervals. Every sound they made echoed.

"This is the Heart of Wolves," Kenver explained in low
tones. Their voice rippled and hummed around them.

Riley swallowed hard and tried to ignore the way the
shadows shifted and pulsed as though the rock itself
were alive.

"Now what?" Aracely's voice boomed. "Whoa, that's
amazing. Echo!"

Echo!

Echo!

Echo!

Aracely's voice called back, seeming to swirl around the room. One voice alone was already powerful. It was going to be even more so when all four of them howled together.

"Lydia, it says you should sit in the center," Riley said, studying Lydia's copy of the rite one last time. "Everyone else spread out. We need to surround her with our calls."

Now Lydia hesitated. Her eyes stuck to the place where she was supposed to sit. It looked harmless enough. Just a curve of sandstone, but all around it, the bowl was scored with gouges. Some were deep, others shallow, all appeared to have been made by claws.

Whatever had happened here in the past, some of it hadn't been pleasant.

"Oh no," Dhonielle muttered.

No, no, no, answered the cave.

Lydia didn't move.

"Lydia?" Riley asked.

"I can do it," Lydia answered softly, but her eyes were trained on the center of the bowl.

She still wasn't moving, and Riley realized it was because she was terrified.

"I'll do it," Riley said. "You don't have to."

That seemed to jar Lydia out of whatever was holding

her back. She shook her head and reached for Riley's hand. "I've got it."

Heat rose in Riley's cheeks at Lydia's touch. Then Lydia let go and stepped down into the bowl. Riley's face felt too hot, her hand too empty, and her thoughts way too jumbled. She wasn't supposed to have these kinds of feelings for perfect Lydia Edgerton, but here they were, making her skin feel funny and distracting her from whatever it was they were here to do.

"Earth to Riley!" Aracely sang.

Lee, lee, lee, the cave sang, too.

Riley cleared her throat and tried to shake the clouds from her brain. "Remember, we're calling to her wolf. Our intentions must be unified, so keep that thought in your mind and keep calling. Lydia, if you need us to stop, just say the word."

"I won't," Lydia promised. "I can do this."

"Okay," Riley said. She wished she could think of something to say that sounded magical. Something that would mark the beginning of the rite the way the greats always did, but she couldn't think of anything, so she settled on, "Let's do this."

Riley began to howl.

Aracely joined in. Her rich voice was throaty and wild, and it resonated around the bowl. Next was Dhonielle. Her call was gentle and high, like birdsong. Kenver was last. Their call was warm and melodic, steady and sure of itself. Gradually their voices grew louder and louder until the sound filled the entire room.

The call thrummed in Riley's chest as though all four voices were coming from inside her. The sandstone dust beneath her fingers vibrated and jumped from the ground. Even her teeth seemed to hum.

Lydia sat with her eyes closed, a very slight crease appearing on her brow. Otherwise, she was quiet and still and showed no signs of distress. Perhaps it wouldn't be so bad; another example of adults overreacting to things.

The call grew a little louder, a little stronger. There was a deeper rumbling note to the chorus now. Riley realized with awe that it was the stone itself, humming like the earth was waking up.

A sound like a small gasp leapt from Lydia's lips and her eyes flew open. One hand clutched at her chest. Riley leaned in, concern and curiosity almost too much to bear. If this worked—if Lydia turned into a wolf right here and now—then they could all finally be real wolves. They could fix this problem all on their own.

Riley drew another breath and pushed her call a little harder, a little louder. The others did the same, their eyes widening as Lydia gasped again and curled down over her knees, one hand pressing against the clawed stone.

Riley looked for any suggestion that Lydia's body was

transforming. A stray tuft of fur, an unusual elongation of her nose, the darkening of her fingernails, but she found none. Not yet, anyway.

Again the call increased. This time, Lydia's cry was so loud, it pierced the cocoon of sound. Now both hands grabbed at her chest, twisting into her shirt like she wanted to tear it apart, but she made no sign for them to stop.

For a moment, everything stayed that way. Then Lydia raised her head sharply and she stared directly at Riley. As if in answer, Riley felt a twist inside her own chest, sharp and swift like someone were compressing her lungs and heart all at once. Like someone had taken ahold of something deep inside her bones and was trying to rip out a part of her. She gasped, fingers digging into the stone, her teeth clamped together, her stomach pinched as pain lanced through her entire body.

The others screamed and groaned, their howl transforming into a collective cry of pain.

The hurt lasted for no more than a few seconds. Then, just as swiftly as it had arrived, it was gone. Riley's muscles unclenched and she could breathe again.

Lydia was huddled on the floor, shivering and whimpering against the stone as waves of pain rippled through her body. Around the room, the others winced and cradled their stomachs. Tears shimmered in Dhonielle's eyes.

Riley slid down the sloped edge to Lydia's side. She was flushed and sweating even while she shivered. Riley smoothed the hair from her forehead. "Are you okay? I'm so sorry," she said.

"It's not your fault," Lydia murmured.

Riley wasn't so sure about that, but now wasn't the time to argue.

"Can you walk?" she asked.

Lydia nodded. She leaned heavily on Riley as the two climbed out of the bowl.

"This way," Kenver whispered, leading them into the tunnels once more.

By the time they reached the entrance, it was nearly dusk. The sun was setting on another day, and they were no closer to being wolves.

He didn't come for us right away. He didn't know we existed. But if he has returned, then he will remember that he was defeated by a group of wolfless children.

You must discover him before he discovers you.

22

A CREATURE OF STORM AND SHADOW

Riley didn't know how long she'd been asleep when she woke to the sound of a growl. It rumbled in her ear as though a wolf were hunched over her, its muzzle pressed against her pillow. She cried out, opening her eyes in terror. Immediately, she wished she hadn't.

She wasn't in her bed at all, but outside. No, not just outside, she realized as a shiver skated down her spine. She was standing in the woods wearing only her pajamas. And she was barefoot.

It was dark. The night air was humid and cold, and as she turned in a slow circle, she realized she had no idea where she was. Nor did she remember leaving her bed or the cabin.

"Hello?" she called into the dark. "Hello?"

An owl hooted, and somewhere in the distance a

branch snapped loudly in half. Riley tried not to imagine something very large stepping on that branch. She tried not to imagine the thing Luke had described, tried not to imagine something waiting to chase her, something that sounded like a storm and smelled like wet leaves. She definitely tried not to imagine that the cold sensation against her skin was the same one Luke had felt before his wolf was stolen.

Another branch snapped and Riley jumped.

Why hadn't she put one of Aracely's light charms into her pocket? Why didn't she sleep with shoes on? Why was this happening?

A dream. Maybe this was a dream. Riley closed her eyes and took three deep breaths, trying to relax. But when she opened her eyes, she was still in the woods.

"Hello?" she called again.

When nothing answered, Riley balled her trembling hands into fists and said, "Move it, Riley."

She picked a direction and started walking. It was slow going without any shoes. The underbrush was thick and weedy, and she took care to make enough noise to scare off any animals hiding beneath the leaves. But after several minutes, she still hadn't found a trail and she felt even more lost than before.

She was just about to nestle down against the trunk of a broad-leafed sycamore and wait until morning when she heard a voice whisper behind her, "Rileeeeey."

She spun around, heart hammering in her chest. But there was no one there.

"Hello?" she managed.

This time, she heard something. But it wasn't her name. It was a wolf call.

A single note, high and piercing, rose from somewhere just ahead. It was both familiar and chilling because that note communicated a very clear message: *Run.*

Riley spun around. She didn't know where she was, much less where she should go, but she started running.

Low branches scraped at her bare legs and vines tugged at her ankles with every step. She stumbled, but she ignored the sting in her knees and kept running.

Soon she heard something crashing through the woods behind her. She ran faster, as fast as she could, until she realized that someone was calling her name.

"Riley! Riley, wait!" the voice called. "Wait for us!"

Riley stopped and turned to find Lydia and Dhonielle darting through the dark woods. Dhonielle's eyes were wide as plates and she clutched one of Aracely's light charms in her hands.

"Are you okay?" Lydia asked.

Riley nodded. "Have you seen anyone else?"

"Just Dhonielle." Lydia's gaze shifted to the woods. "Do you remember how you got here?"

Riley shook her head, then stopped. "Do you hear that?" she asked.

It was a song, soft but definitely nearby, and the voice was familiar.

They recognized it at the same time. "Aracely!"

They hurried toward the lullaby and found Aracely perched on top of a fallen tree trunk with the lithocharm cupped in her hands. She stopped its song when she spotted them.

"Hi!" she called cheerfully, as though waking up alone in the woods had done nothing to diminish her good mood. "Is everyone okay? Isn't this weird? My older sister Johanna used to sleepwalk when she was little, and one time they found her outside in the doghouse! This is kind of like that."

"She's fine," Lydia confirmed.

"Where's Kenver?" Riley asked.

They fanned out, calling in the dark for Kenver, but received no answer.

"Oh no. What if something happened to them?" Dhonielle asked.

"Maybe they're just back at the cabin?" Lydia didn't sound like she believed her own suggestion. If the four of them were here, so was Kenver.

"Dhonielle, hold that light up high," Riley instructed.

Dhonielle raised her arm, letting the little light shine against the black trees.

Another wolf call sounded in the distance. The message still frightfully clear: *Run.*

But run from what? Run where? And they couldn't leave without Kenver.

"What if something *else* sees the light?" Dhonielle whispered, her voice trembling. "Maybe we should just hide."

"KEEEEENVEEER!" Aracely shouted.

"Shhh!" Lydia clamped a hand over Aracely's mouth as Dhonielle shrieked and dropped the charm. The light went out immediately.

"Oh no! I lost it! I lost it!" Dhonielle shuffled through the leaves and dirt but the stone was gone.

Just behind that sound was another. A rustling and slapping noise. And it was getting closer.

And closer.

"Be quiet," Riley hissed, but it was too late.

A figure crashed through the bushes next to them, landing in their midst.

Aracely screamed. Dhonielle wilted. Lydia ducked. Riley raised her fists.

And Kenver gasped for air. "I thought—I was—alone!"

"Kenver! You scared us to death!" Aracely caught Kenver in a hug. "Well, Dhonielle might actually be dead. But the rest of us are good."

Kenver gave a weak smile, but the fear was written plainly on their face.

Another wolf call pierced the night air, much closer than the one before. Right on its heels came the sound of wolves racing through the woods.

Riley spotted them almost as soon as she heard them. In the distance, wolves darted above the underbrush like dolphins arcing out of water. They were running at full speed, silent and panicked.

They were running away from something.

"What is that?" Aracely asked.

Behind the pack, something moved in the dark. It rolled between the trees like a storm, shadows and light twisting in the shape of a giant wolf. Much larger than a normal wolf. A breeze blew toward them, bringing with it the scent of wet leaves and something electric. They gasped.

"Oh no," Kenver whispered, while Dhonielle began to emit a high-pitched noise.

"The Devourer," Aracely said, and no one disagreed.

"He's real," Lydia added.

The beast moved languidly, its powerful gait unhurried as it pursued the racing wolves. Somehow, in spite of not running, it was right on top of the pack.

Older wolves might be able to outrun it, but the younger ones were falling behind.

"He's going to catch them," Lydia said, her voice low and hard. "He's going to do it again."

"We have to do something!" Aracely added.

Riley knew both things were true. But what could they do? Her heart knocked against her ribs, making it hard to think. She took a deep breath and reminded herself not to panic. That was Rule #1: *Don't panic, plan it.*

The older wolves were running hard, carving a path for the pups to follow. But the younger wolves were getting tired. Riley watched in horror as three of the smallest wolves drifted a little too far from the rest of the pack, falling behind where the adults could no longer see them.

That was exactly what the creature was waiting for. It coiled its body, and in a movement so swift Riley had trouble tracking it, it sliced across their path, cutting them off from the pack. The three young wolves yipped in terror, swerving away from the beast and running as hard as they could in the opposite direction. But their new path took them even farther from the pack and they were already exhausted.

"Come on!" Riley called, still not sure what she intended to do.

The others followed, racing through the dark woods as fast as their bare feet could take them. It wasn't enough. They simply could not run as fast as real wolves.

On instinct, Riley reached for Lydia's hand on one side and Dhonielle's on the other. Then, reaching for her magic, she whistled. The sound was so sharp and so loud, it surprised even her.

Instantly, the three wolves turned toward Riley and the others.

"Yes!" Riley cried.

"Um . . ." Dhonielle added.

"Claws and teeth!" Lydia exclaimed as the beast slowly turned toward them as well. "He's coming this way!"

His muzzle was inky black, and his lips peeled back to reveal bone-white teeth. His eyes were like yellow crescent moons curved around black pupils. His body was massive and seemed to roil and flash like a thunderstorm. And as a low growl rumbled through the trees, the earthy, sweet scent of decaying leaves wafted over them.

"I think we should run!" Aracely called, already stumbling backward.

"It's . . . he's not after us," Kenver managed, their voice stiffened by fear.

A plan. Riley needed a plan. If the beast wasn't after them, then maybe she could do something.

"We have to stop him!" she shouted.

Though every part of her was trembling, Riley ran toward the looming wolf. She kept her eyes on the three small wolves ahead of her, hoping they could keep running just a little bit longer.

When she was close enough, she stopped, planted her feet, and released the loudest wolf call she could, trying with all her might to push the beast back.

He snarled and snapped at the air, flinching away from the sound. Riley's heart leapt at the sight. She howled harder, but this time he was ready for her. He crouched, body flashing with light. Then he turned his yellow eyes on her and dove forward with a snarl.

Riley braced for an impact.

But the hit never came.

Instead, one of the wolves dove between her and the beast, protecting her from the attack. Riley heard a sickening *thunk* as the Devourer rammed its massive head into the little wolf, knocking it to the ground with a whimper.

Before the other two could make their escape, the Devourer spotted them and howled, catching them up in a sticky web of magic and pulling them back.

Now all three were at the beast's mercy.

Riley's call turned into a scream, a shout. "Hey! Over here! Over here!"

But it was no use. As Riley watched, the storm that roiled inside the creature's body stretched to engulf the three wolves. Their bodies rose from the ground and they whimpered in pain as their paws scrabbled at the air.

There was a flash of blue light and then the storm receded like a wave into the ocean.

When it was gone, so was the beast.

And on the ground not far from where Riley stood were three kids—one that made Riley's heart squeeze painfully against her chest.

"Milo!"

23

THE LONG WALK HOME

For a moment, Riley could only stare at the shape of her little brother lying on the forest floor. Milo shivered and breathed. Then he began to cry.

His cries rang out in the empty woods, the only sound in the aftermath of the attack.

Riley rushed forward, but the rest of the young pack was there first, cutting her off. The older wolves arrived a moment later, racing back to the scene. They circled the three kids, pressing their muzzles against their bare shoulders and cheeks.

A pain squeezed in Riley's throat as she fully understood what had happened. Milo's wolf had been stripped away. Just like Luke's. Just like Paislee's.

Footsteps approached from behind.

"Dhonielle?!"

The voice startled all of them. Even the wolves raised their heads.

Aunt Alexis was approaching through the trees.

"Dhonielle! Riley! What are you two doing here?"

Riley thought back to the moment she'd awoken in the woods. There was no explanation she could offer that would make any sense.

"It's Milo," she offered instead, feeling tears burn in her eyes. "He got Milo."

"Who did?" Aunt Alexis turned her attention to Milo and the other two.

"The . . . the Devouring Wolf!" That was twice in one day that she'd said the name aloud to an adult, but any doubt she'd had about it before was gone. He'd been here. In the woods. Surely someone else had seen him.

But Aunt Alexis shook her head. "I know you're upset, but there's no such thing."

Riley gaped at her aunt. "Didn't you see him?!"

"I don't know what I saw," she said, stripping her jacket off and hurrying forward. "Henry, Micah."

Two of the adult wolves shimmered and transformed at her command, each gathering one of the crying pups into their arms.

Once again, Aunt Alexis wasn't with her prime. There was no sign of Mama C, Crow, Kat, or Nic. It was strange, but everything about what had happened tonight was strange.

"It's okay," Aunt Alexis murmured as Milo pressed a tearstained face against her shoulder. "You're safe. I've got you."

Riley didn't think anything was okay, but the words seemed to calm Milo down a little.

"He can have my pullover," Aracely offered, tugging the cotton shrug over her buns.

Aunt Alexis shifted Milo and dressed him in Aracely's purple pullover, using her own jacket as a makeshift skirt. The whole time, Milo stared at the ground while tears streamed down his cheeks.

A few more adult wolves arrived, nosing swiftly through the brush. They remained long enough to assess the situation, then several took off for Clawroot while others led the young wolves away.

Riley wanted to let Milo know that she was here. But she didn't know what to say or how to say it, so she didn't say anything. She just stood close enough that if Milo looked up, he'd at least find a friendly face. Someone who would believe him when he described what had happened tonight. But Milo didn't look up. Not even when Aunt Alexis lifted him in strong arms and began to carry him out of the woods.

They followed Aunt Alexis in silence, glad that she at least seemed to know where they were in relation to Clawroot. After a while, Milo's sobs turned into sniffles and hiccups and then nothing. Riley wondered if he'd fallen asleep.

By the time they crossed the wards into Clawroot, Riley was more alarmed than ever. How had she managed to go so deep into the woods without waking up?

Judging by the looks the others gave her, they were just as curious and just as concerned.

The village was full of light and motion. As soon as they'd been spotted, Mama C hurried out to meet them.

"Alexis?" she asked, with a frown that was equal parts suspicion and irritation. "What were you doing out there? I thought I told you to get some—Milo?"

"I was doing what you told us to do: protect the young. But we're not protecting them, CeCe. This time it was three at once!" Alexis answered without stopping. "Where's Dr. Khorram?"

"Ready and waiting in the hall." Mama C's response was tense, and when her eyes fell on Riley, the frown on her face deepened. "What were *you* doing out there?"

"Um, we, um," Riley started, wishing she could fumble her way into an answer that wouldn't make her mom mad. Wishing even more that she could just tell her mom that she'd seen the Devouring Wolf with her own eyes without risking another public reprimand. Maybe if Bethany Books were here, Riley could convince her. Instead, Riley settled on the same answer she'd given Aunt Alexis. "We don't really know."

Mama C's frown became a glare. "Now is not the time to be coy. I told you—all of you—to stay in Clawroot, and at the first opportunity you disobeyed me."

"I'm not being coy," Riley shot back. "We really don't

know how we got out there. We were asleep and then we were awake, only instead of being in our beds, we were in the woods."

Aunt Alexis was gone now, as were the other wolves. It was just the six of them and the waning moon high overhead.

Mama C studied Riley as she digested this new information. If the look on her face was any indication, it wasn't sitting well. She thought Riley was lying to her. Trying to avoid getting into trouble for leaving Clawroot again. And the problem was, Riley couldn't prove that wasn't the case.

"I'm not lying," she promised.

"She's not," Lydia echoed, stepping up beside Riley. The others stepped up silently, adding their support to hers.

Riley felt something warm bloom inside her. It gave her just enough courage to keep going.

"Mom, I promise, something is happening to us. We don't know what or how, but we know it's connected to—" She stopped herself again. Her mom had been furious the first time she'd mentioned the Devouring Wolf. She needed to work her way back up to it. "Why we haven't shifted yet," she finished.

"So." Mama C did not look convinced, but Riley still had hope. "You're all saying that you didn't leave your cabin tonight? You just mysteriously ended up in the woods? And you think it has something to do with your condition?"

Riley held her breath and nodded.

She wasn't worried about getting into trouble anymore because they were already in trouble. Big trouble. What they needed now was help. And if anyone could do it, it was Great Callahan.

But Riley's heart sank when Mama C shook her head and said four terrible words: "I don't believe you."

24

CAN YOU HEAR ME NOW?

The next day, every one of them had small cuts on their feet, their arms and legs, and in Aracely's case, even her face, all from running through the dark woods. They were covered in Band-Aids and bruises, they were still confused about how they'd ended up out there in the first place, and all of that was in addition to the fact that Great Callahan thought they were liars.

They were grumpy to begin with, but the real argument started when Riley suggested they sneak away to the archive to search for more information about the Devouring Wolf.

"Riley, just stop!" Dhonielle threw her pillow down for emphasis. It was covered in a pink satin pillowcase that she'd brought from home and stood out against the patchwork red-and-blue quilt on her bed. "We're in enough trouble as it is. You're just going to get us into more."

"We're in exactly as much trouble as we were," Riley

protested. "And besides, last night wasn't even my fault."

"It was terrifying, though." Kenver's eyes darted nervously toward the window and the woods beyond. "I don't want anything like that to happen again. I woke up all alone. I thought—I thought you'd all left me."

"We wouldn't do that, but that's another reason we should keep digging." It seemed so obvious to Riley that the only way to stop things like that from happening was to learn more about them. Why didn't the others agree?

"You're pushing too hard. We're just kids," Dhonielle said, sounding like Uncle Will.

"We're twelve!" Riley threw up her hands in exasperation. "We're practically teenagers! That's not kids!"

"But it's not an adult," Lydia interjected. She looked especially tired with dark rings beneath her brown eyes. "We should let the adults figure this out and just stay put."

Why is Riley always so bossy?

Riley felt her jaw drop. Had someone actually said that? Or had she imagined it?

"The adults aren't figuring it out. They won't even listen to us!" she said.

"That doesn't change the fact that we're too young to go up against someone as powerful as the Devouring Wolf. If that's even who it is," said Lydia.

"What do you mean, 'if'?" Riley was getting upset now. She'd thought they were all on the same page.

"Don't fight, okay?" Aracely was seated on her bed with a massive stuffed cat clutched against her chest.

"We're not fighting. I just mean we might be overlooking the simplest explanation. It's more likely that someone is doing the same things the Devouring Wolf did than that the same guy has come back," Lydia explained.

Riley deflated a little. Lydia was doing it again. She was stepping into the middle of things like the natural leader, pushing Riley out.

"That's even more reason for us to stay put. The adults will figure it out," Aracely said confidently. "That's what they do."

Wow. Aracely is so naive sometimes.

Riley blinked. Had that voice been different from the first?

"But no matter what, that doesn't change anything," Riley said. She hated the way her voice sounded different when she got upset like this. It sounded like she was on the verge of tears. "Either way, there's something—or someone—out there stealing wolves from our pack and they're all looking for the wrong thing. We have to do something about that."

Ugh. I just want all of this to stop already!

"Dhonielle, it isn't going to stop just because you want it to!" Riley snapped.

Dhonielle's mouth fell open.

All of their mouths fell open and Riley slowly realized

two things. The first was that she was talking back to a voice in her head. The second was that she wasn't the only one who had heard it.

"Whoa. I thought I was imagining it, but . . . that was real?" Aracely asked.

And then her voice echoed thinly in Riley's mind, saying, *Can you hear me now?*

Everyone looked at Aracely and nodded.

"Whoa," she repeated.

"My thoughts exactly," Kenver said.

"We can . . . talk to each other . . . telepathically." Lydia spread out her sentence as if she were talking to herself more than to them.

"How?" Aracely asked, the same instant Kenver said, "Why?"

"Because of the Devourer!" Riley jumped up in excitement. "Remember what Dhonielle found in that story? When the Devouring Wolf rose up, five wolves didn't transform. That's it. That's us."

Dhonielle nodded, then recited, "'When the Devourer rose, siphoning more power than a single wolf should possess, all magic shifted. The most extreme example was five young wolves whose transformations were stunted. In the story they were called saplings.'"

"Saplings," Kenver said. "I like that."

"Was there anything else?" Lydia asked.

Dhonielle only shook her head. "It was just a story."

"Seems like more than a story now," Kenver said thoughtfully.

Saplings. Little Saps. Sap, Sap, Sapling Pack. Oooh! Aracely's voice trotted along.

"Sapling Pack," Kenver said, laughing. "That's a good name for us. It's gender neutral and everything."

"Oh, sorry. Wow. I'm going to have to figure out when my thoughts are just my thoughts and when they're brain words or whatever. How did you remember that anyway? You read that days ago and you could just repeat it." Aracely's voice was uncharacteristically subdued.

"I just do. I like words and sometimes they stick with me. Sort of the way you remember the lyrics to a song." Dhonielle shrugged sheepishly.

"But why can we hear each other now when we couldn't before?" Lydia asked.

Oooh, good question. Aracely's voice popped into Riley's mind again.

This time they all laughed.

"Sorry! I'm so sorry!" Aracely slapped a hand to her forehead. "I'm going to need a foil hat or something. Like immediately. You don't even know how many random thoughts I have in a day. Especially about dinosaurs. I'm like a thinkasaurus."

It did seem like the kind of thing they were going to have to figure out. And fast. But right now, Riley was mostly concerned with Lydia's question: Why now?

"Maybe it's connected to last night?" Riley suggested. "The way we were all pulled out of bed together and drawn into the woods?"

"Could just be that our magic is developing differently since we didn't transform," Dhonielle suggested.

That did make good sense, but Riley felt like they were still missing something.

"If we're connected to the Devourer, it could have something to do with him." Kenver fiddled with their camera, pointing it at various spots in the room and snapping pictures at random.

Riley thought about that. Last night, the Devourer had taken three wolves at once and a few hours later, they'd started hearing each other. Had anything happened after Luke lost his wolf? Or Paislee?

Riley leapt up from her bed. "The dream!"

"What about it?" Lydia asked.

"It happened after Paislee lost her wolf. And before that we all heard the second growl. That had to be when Luke was losing his wolf. Now Milo and the others lost their wolves, and this happens," she explained, feeling breathless. "I think . . . I think it's possible that every time the Devourer steals someone's wolf, we all get a little stronger, too."

"Because we're connected." Kenver's eyes were wide with alarm.

"Yes!" Riley nearly shouted. "Because we're connected!"

Riley felt the same way she did when she finally solved a difficult math problem, all the pieces and numbers coming together in just the right way.

"To the Devouring Wolf." Dhonielle's fear was palpable. It sucked Riley's excitement away, leaving her with the same cold dread she saw in her cousin's eyes.

"To the Devouring Wolf," she repeated.

That definitely didn't feel good.

"What about the first growl?" Lydia asked

"What about it?" Riley asked.

"Well, it happened right before the Full Moon Rite, so it must be what connected the five of us in the first place. Right?"

"That could be," Riley agreed, still not sure what Lydia was getting at.

"So." Lydia paused to lick her lips, her big brown eyes skating nervously from face to face before she continued. "So whose wolf did he take then?"

The question made Riley's breath catch in her throat. The implications were chilling. None of the tenderfoot pups had been at Wax & Wayne that early in the day. Only the adults. And according to them, nothing strange had happened before the Full Moon Rite. None of the wards had been broken.

Which could only mean one thing.

Riley swallowed hard and looked at the rest of the group as horror slunk down her spine.

Then she licked her lips and said, "The Devouring Wolf has been inside the wards all along."

There is something you need to know, and this is of the greatest importance: the Devourer can change his appearance.

Once he has stolen someone's wolf, he can assume their likeness. He can look like someone close to you and you would never know the difference.

Stay vigilant, my friends. Do not let him deceive you.

25

THE VISITOR

They opened the door just as Bethany Books raised her hand to knock on it.

"Good morning, pups!" Behind her blue-rimmed glasses her eyes were wide and warm. "I was just coming to, well, to discuss things with you. Can I come in?"

Bethany took a seat on one of the two chairs, leaving the little sofa for the rest of them. Riley sat between Dhonielle and Lydia, while Kenver perched birdlike on one arm and Aracely straddled the other.

"I've brought breakfast for you." She set a canvas sack on the coffee table between them and placed a second on the floor by her feet.

"Why can't we just go to the dining hall?" Riley asked, suspicion creeping into her voice.

"Oh, well, because you're all grounded, of course," Bethany said brightly, adjusting her glasses.

"But why?" Aracely asked. "We told Great Callahan that we didn't mean to leave the cabin last night. It happened *to* us, not because of us. We shouldn't be in trouble for that."

"Mmhmm, last night was . . . confusing. But the point remains that you were out of your cabin when you shouldn't have been, and now we're going to make sure you stay put."

Bethany's smile vanished and she was suddenly, uncharacteristically serious.

"And as part of your punishment, you're going to clean this cabin from nose to tail." She nudged the sack at her feet. "I've got all the cleaning supplies here that you'll need."

Riley sighed in relief. They'd only been here for a few days. The cabin wasn't that dirty and wouldn't take long to clean. Nothing in the whole place could compare to the travesty that was four filthy litter boxes.

"And when you're done with that," Bethany said, breaking into Riley's thoughts. "You can each write me a paper on why it was wrong of you to leave Clawroot. Two pages. Handwritten."

"Two pages?!" Aracely erupted. "How am I supposed to say I was wrong for two whole pages?!"

Bethany smiled again, adjusting her glasses. "Figuring that out is part of the point."

"Where's my mom?" Riley asked.

"They've resumed their search of the woods and will be gone all day. It's just you and me here."

"But the Dev—OW!" Lydia had pinched Riley in the thigh. Riley glared but decided on a different approach. "But there's something out there. Shouldn't they bring the young wolves here? To keep them safe?"

Bethany hesitated, adjusting her glasses for the third time. It was as if she wasn't used to them. "You're right. There is something out there and it is clearly inside our wards. The young wolves can't transform without risking their magic, so we've moved them to Cottonwood Hollow and set up a watch for that very reason. No witch or hunter will get near them again."

That would be great if a witch or a hunter were the one after them and not, oh, I don't know, only the biggest boogeyman in all of history! Aracely's voice echoed loudly in Riley's mind. Even Lydia flinched a little. They definitely had to figure out a way to control this.

They're sitting ducks out there. Kenver looked at Riley, eyes wide and urgent.

"I know it must feel like we've forgotten what's happening to you, but we haven't. As soon as we've cleared the woods of any danger, you'll have our full attention once more. We *will* figure this out," Bethany said, misinterpreting their silence.

Should we tell her? Dhonielle asked.

One part of Riley wanted to. Maybe Bethany would be more sympathetic than Mama C had been. But Riley couldn't quit thinking about what they'd just discovered;

that the Devouring Wolf had been here all along. That meant he must have had help. From within the pack itself.

No, Riley answered.

Dhonielle squirmed in her seat. On Riley's other side Lydia brushed her fingertips against Riley's leg. The gesture sent shivers racing up and down Riley's back while heat flooded her cheeks. She lost complete track of the conversation for a moment.

Having delivered their sentence of imprisonment, Bethany stood to leave. "I'll be back to check on you in a bit."

"What about Milo?" Riley blurted.

Bethany pulled the door open, then paused. "He's doing as well as can be expected."

"Can I—can we come visit him?" Riley asked.

A kind smile appeared on Bethany's face and she nodded. "You get this cabin clean and write me a paper and then you can visit him."

"Thank you," Riley said as Bethany shut the door behind her.

"I really hate writing papers," Aracely complained. "They take so many words!"

"Well, I hate cleaning," Riley admitted. "But I bet we can do it all together."

For the next two hours, they scrubbed the bathroom and swept the floors and scribbled ideas for their papers.

It turned out working as a team made everything go faster.

As they cleaned, they practiced speaking to each other in their minds. At first it was nearly impossible to tell when a thought was just a thought and when they were projecting it to the others. But after a while, it got a little easier.

Aracely was still very loud, Dhonielle still very soft, and Kenver very grumpy even in their mind, but they'd all gotten the hang of when to project and when to with-hold. By that time, the work was done and Bethany Books was knocking on their door once more. As promised, she'd come to check on their progress, and she was so pleased that she let them go to the dining hall for lunch.

"And after lunch, you can visit Milo," she said. "He's awake, and as long as he's up for it, Dr. Khorram says it's okay if he has visitors."

After that, Riley couldn't move fast enough. She scarfed an entire sandwich and apple in the time it took the others to eat half as much. One look at her anxious face, however, and they picked up the pace.

Bethany led them to the next to last cabin in the row, cabin five. Riley was only a little surprised to find Luke waiting for them on the porch.

"Bethany said—well, I was hoping you wouldn't mind if I joined you," Luke said. "I thought they might like to, you know, talk."

Riley had almost forgotten that it wasn't just Milo in the cabin. Three pups had lost their wolves last night.

"Of course," she said.

Dr. Khorram opened the door for them. He was a middle-aged man with no hair and brown eyes that were as sharp as an eagle's. In contrast, his nose was rounded and long, ending above plump lips that smiled easily. He was dressed in a button-down and incredibly tight pants.

"Come on in," he said. "I'll see if Milo's ready for visitors."

They stood in a semicircle, trying to be as quiet as possible. Dr. Khorram's voice was muffled by the bedroom door.

Riley hated to think of her brother in pain and wished she could do something—anything—to make it better. She was ready to barge through the door when Dr. Khorram reappeared and caught her by the shoulders.

"I'm sorry, Riley, but Milo's feeling a little overwhelmed right now." He paused and looked apologetic before he added, "But he would like to see you." Dr. Khorram turned to Luke.

Riley took a horrified step back.

"Did you—did you tell him it was me?" she asked.

"I'm afraid so," Dr. Khorram answered. "I'm sure he'll want to see you eventually."

Riley didn't understand what was happening. Milo was her brother. He didn't even know Luke.

Then all at once she realized that he must blame her for what happened. The beast had been coming for her when Milo intervened. He must blame her for losing his wolf.

He must hate her for it.

Luke took a tentative step forward. "I'm sorry, Riley," he said, then he followed Dr. Khorram inside.

It was the Full Moon Rite all over again, only this time, Milo wasn't leaving her behind because he had to but because he wanted to. Because he was going through something she couldn't understand.

Not a real wolf, the voice in the back of her mind whispered sharply.

The lump in Riley's throat was turning into a boulder. She spun on her heel and hurried out of the cabin, taking deep breaths of fresh air to hold back her tears.

The others followed. She could hear Lydia saying her name, trying to get her to stop. But all Riley could hear in her head was that same haunting refrain: *Not a wolf, not a wolf, not a real wolf.*

Riley, stop!

She stopped, caught off guard by Lydia's voice in her head.

Before she could move again, the others had her surrounded. Dhonielle looked nervous and Aracely concerned, and Kenver was sporting a fierce scowl. Lydia took Riley's hand and held it tightly.

"Don't leave us like that," Lydia said, braiding their fingers together in a way that made Riley feel warm all over. "We're here for you."

Riley swallowed hard. The threat of tears was fading, but the pain was still tight in her chest.

"I just . . . thought he'd want to see me," she admitted.

"He will," Lydia promised. "Remember how mad you were a few nights ago? He's just really confused and angry right now."

"He's probably embarrassed, too," Dhonielle suggested. "I was with everyone looking at us that night of the Full Moon Rite."

It was hard to ignore the truth of all of those things. Riley had been so angry and confused and embarrassed that she'd told her mom that she wasn't a real wolf. And she hadn't even apologized.

Remembering didn't make her feel good. She may have been angry when she said it, but she only said it because part of her believed it was true. Part of her had believed that the only way to be a real wolf was to be born one. To transform on the night of the first full moon of summer.

But if that was true, then Riley would never be a real wolf, and she didn't like how that felt either.

Milo must be feeling just as angry and confused, and she shouldn't be mad at him for not wanting to see her. Even if it hurt.

"Okay," she agreed. "We'll try again later."

They were halfway back when Riley spotted someone skulking around behind their cabin.

Wait, she said, pulling the others to a stop and pointing toward the shadowy figure.

Who is that? Aracely asked.

They watched as the figure stooped down and buried something in the ground, stomping the earth flat with their foot. When they looked up again, Riley caught a glimpse of their face and nearly gasped.

"Mom?" Dhonielle asked too softly for anyone but the five of them to hear.

Aunt Alexis stomped at the ground a few more times, then turned to leave. At the sight of them, she stopped.

"Pups!" she said, sounding very surprised. "I thought you were inside."

"We were visiting Milo," Dhonielle explained.

A frown landed on Aunt Alexis's lips and she shifted her gaze to Riley. "How is he?"

Riley didn't want to admit that he hadn't wanted to see her, so she shrugged. "Not great."

Aunt Alexis nodded, then shook her head. "He'll get better. A little bit every day."

She didn't mean that he would magically recover, but that he would get used to it. That didn't sound better to Riley.

"What are you doing?" Aracely managed to ask it without sounding accusatory. "What are you burying there?"

"Ah." Aunt Alexis brushed her palms against her pants and took a few steps toward them. She still looked and sounded a little tired. "It's a protection ward. To keep you all a little extra safe."

"Isn't Clawroot safe already?" Kenver asked shrewdly.

Aunt Alexis pursed her lips before answering. "It is. But so was Wax & Wayne, and something got in anyway. This is just in case." She stepped forward to pull Dhonielle into a hug. "Just in case."

"Thanks, Mom," Dhonielle murmured, leaning into the hug.

"But," Riley started, following a suspicious thought, "why aren't you out with the others? Why aren't you with your prime?" *Again,* she added silently.

"Just following orders and getting some rest." Aunt Alexis let Dhonielle go with a tight smile. "I'll be around if you need me, okay?"

"Okay," Dhonielle confirmed.

The others filed into the cabin, but Riley hung back to watch as Aunt Alexis walked away. Then, just before she turned the corner, Aunt Alexis looked over her shoulder and smiled directly at Riley.

26

A VERY INSISTENT DIARY

Inside the cabin, Riley found everyone standing very, very still.

"What is—" Before she could finish the question, a voice whispered inside her head, *Riley.*

The voice wasn't one Riley recognized.

Kenver, it whispered again.

Aracely, Dhonielle, Lydia.

"Who's doing that?" Dhonielle stepped closer to Riley, hands clenched tight together.

"Could we be hearing someone else's thoughts?" Lydia asked.

"Like the Devouring Wolf?!" Aracely hopped on her toes like she was about to explode.

"Maybe," Kenver said thoughtfully. "But I don't think so."

Riley, the voice called again. Then again. *Riley. Kenver. Aracely. Dhonielle. Lydia.* Over and over in a loop that got faster and faster in a discordant jumble. It sounded like they were surrounded, like people were hidden inside the walls of the cabin. But there was no one there.

"What is happening?" Dhonielle's shoulders were hunched up around her ears, her eyes darting frantically around the room.

"Is it magic?" Aracely asked, turning to Kenver for confirmation.

"Obviously," Kenver said. "But what is causing it?"

"I think it's coming from the bedroom," Lydia suggested, though she made no move to investigate.

The sounds were haunting, terrifying, but something about them also felt familiar. Riley moved toward the bedroom door and very carefully stepped inside.

The whispers grew louder, and they were all coming from the same direction.

Dhonielle! Lydia! they said. And then, *Willa! Ruth! Eudora!*

"It's coming from over there." Lydia pointed over Riley's shoulder toward Kenver's bed.

Though the whispers were inside their heads, and Riley still wasn't totally sure how that worked, they came with a sense of direction. And Lydia was right. They were coming from Kenver's bed.

Riley took another step into the room. Lydia moved with her on one side, Dhonielle on the other, and the other two close behind.

Annabeth! Grace!

The whispers grew louder as they approached Kenver's bed, until they were so loud, Riley could hardly think. But there, resting atop Kenver's neatly folded quilt, was the old leather-bound journal they'd pilfered from the archive with the letters *G. B.* clearly embossed on the cover.

Riley's hand shook as she reached for it, but the second her fingers curled around the soft spine, the whispers stopped.

"What do you think it wants?" Aracely asked.

"It's a journal; how can it want anything?" Lydia pressed in next to Riley.

"It's enspelled," Kenver explained. "I think it wanted us to find it."

The group huddled around Riley in a tight circle. Kenver reached out to touch the cover. Aracely followed suit. As if following an unspoken command, Lydia and Dhonielle were next.

And suddenly they weren't in the room anymore, but in a clearing standing around a large stone that glittered in the dim light of the moon.

"Grace!" someone shouted. "Grace, now!"

Riley turned to see a young girl in an old-fashioned dress that fell all the way to the ground. Her eyes were bright blue, her hair a reddish orange that curled at her milk-pale cheeks, and she was staring directly into Riley's eyes.

"The stone," she said urgently. "The stone is the lock, but you are the key."

"What does that mean?" Riley asked.

But it was as if the girl didn't understand the question. Behind her, the others were calling her name. The wind picked up and the stone began to glow as an ominous growl rumbled around them.

"Read the diary," she said. "I wrote it for you."

There was a flash of light and then they were back in the cabin with the journal held between them.

"Um," Aracely said.

"Great moons!" Lydia nearly shouted.

"I think we'd better see what's inside this thing," Dhonielle added.

"But it was blank," Kenver reminded them.

Riley opened the book and let the pages flip past. At first, it was just as Kenver said, empty page after empty page, but as they watched, ink began to appear, crawling across the previously blank pages until they were filled.

Without another word, they began to read, their faces pressed cheek to cheek.

I have enspelled this diary so that it will only respond to your touch when all five of you are together. It is the only way I know to ensure this information reaches you safely.

You did not transform so that you could fight. Wolf magic is vulnerable because it is constantly in motion. It wants to change and run, and that is how he is able to steal it. Your magic is still firmly rooted inside you. It cannot be taken against your will.

Even so, his power is too great to destroy. The witch who tricked him made sure of that, so we bound him in stone, where he could do no harm.

If he has escaped, then something has gone wrong. I'm afraid I cannot help you with that except to say that if it worked once, it can work again. The stone is a prison in want of a prisoner; you must return him to it.

The only way for you to succeed is to stay together. Fight together. Your strength and true power are each other.

"We were right!" Aracely jumped up from the sofa, her curls bouncing even higher. "The Devouring Wolf is real, and since he can look like anyone, he's probably been right in front of us the whole time! This is great!"

"Two things," Kenver said with a scowl. "One, he can only look like someone if he's already taken their wolf, and two, we need to reevaluate your definition of *great*, because I think you might have a problem."

"We definitely have a problem," Dhonielle muttered.

Riley felt her stomach flop as she understood her cousin's point. "Exactly who is the Devouring Wolf?" she asked.

"If he can only look like someone when he's stolen their wolf, then he can only be Luke, right?" Aracely asked. "He was the first one, and he's been in Clawroot the whole time."

"But Luke wasn't the first, remember?" Lydia countered. "The first time we all heard a growl was the day of the Full Moon Rite. That was the first wolf he stole, and we still don't know who that might have been."

"So." Kenver sounded tentative, like they didn't really want to say what they were about to say. "Who do we think it is?"

No one volunteered a name.

"Has anyone been acting strangely recently?" Lydia asked.

Another uncomfortable silence followed. It had to be someone who could have gone missing around the Full Moon Rite. Someone who had been nearby when Luke, Paislee, and the others all lost their wolves. Someone who wasn't acting like themselves.

Riley nearly dropped the book as she realized who it was.

"One person," she said.

All eyes turned to her.

She cleared her throat, suddenly uneasy being the center of their attention. "Well," she started. "There's one person who's been prowling around at night, showing up where no one expects her to be, and going against her alpha's orders."

"Who?!" Aracely shrieked.

Riley glanced at her cousin. "Aunt Alexis."

Dhonielle sprang to her feet, panic flashing in her eyes. "My mom? You think something happened to my mom?!"

"Maybe," Riley said, but now that'd she'd made the connection, it felt like more than a mere possibility. "Think about it. If she found the Devourer's stone and he caught her, then he would need a cover story for the rest of the prime pack."

"The hunters' snare," Kenver said.

"Exactly. What if there was never any snare at all,

but the Devourer needed everyone to think there was to explain why he—Aunt Alexis—was acting so strange. Avoiding her prime, prowling around our cabin, and she was nearby when Milo's wolf was taken."

"But"—Dhonielle swallowed hard—"wouldn't I know if she wasn't my mom? I mean, shouldn't I just know?"

"Maybe if you were around her more," Lydia said in her soothing way. "But you've only seen her a few times since this all started."

"And we don't even know for sure if it's her," Kenver added. "This is just a theory."

"Yeah, it could also be Bethany Books, if you think about it," Aracely said.

"You think so?" Dhonielle looked relieved to be considering someone else.

"Sure! Isn't it weird that no one has found any information about all this by now? She's the one reading all the books, which means she controls what we see and what we don't," Aracely said, sounding shockingly rational for once. "She could have found all the answers by now. Maybe she has! And if she's the Devourer, she's probably burned it all up so we'll never know."

"That is . . . chilling," Kenver said, and Riley had to agree. It hadn't even occurred to Riley to be suspicious of Bethany's lack of helpful information, but now that Aracely said it, it *was* strange.

"Of course, we can't be sure." Lydia hurried to keep things calm. "Right now, all we know is that we don't know who to trust, so this is up to us. We have to keep the diary a secret."

"What's a secret?"

All five of them spun toward the door. Bethany Books stood there, having come in while they were all distracted. She smiled sweetly, holding out a tray of cupcakes.

"Sorry. I didn't mean to startle you. I figured you could all use a little pick-me-up."

Riley stared blankly at the tray and the woman behind it. Bethany had been around just as much as anyone else. She had access to all of Wax & Wayne. And none of them knew her well enough to say whether or not her recent behavior was stranger than usual. It was just as likely that it was her as it was Aunt Alexis.

One glance at Dhonielle, and Riley knew she was having the same thoughts.

You're all acting a little too suspicious. Kenver's voice was a snap in Riley's mind.

With a big smile, Kenver took the tray. "You never have to apologize for cupcakes."

The cupcakes were chocolate with chocolate icing. In other words, they were perfect. After a few bites, Riley felt like she was recovering her senses, and her senses reminded her that Bethany Books had been at the Full Moon Rite with the rest of them.

For a brief second, Riley considered sharing everything with her—from the journal to their suspicions about Aunt Alexis—but she stopped herself. It was just like Grace had written in her diary: they could only trust each other.

27

THE DEVOURING WOLF

When Riley was little, Mama C had told her that part of being a wolf was being connected to nature. Wolf senses would make her more sensitive to changes in the weather and to changes in her own body.

"If you ever feel disconnected from yourself or like you're having trouble getting your mind to settle into your body, then it's time to get outside and breathe in the sun, the moon, and the stars."

Riley tossed and turned so late into the night that she eventually gave up on sleep altogether and went to sit on the porch. Dark clouds blanketed the sky. What little moonlight made it through was ghostly, painting the forest in shadows that swayed back and forth.

Riley breathed in the cool night air and tried not to think about anything. But it was too hard, and soon she was thinking of everything she'd read in Grace Barley's diary. She'd been right all along. The Devouring Wolf was real. Not only that, but according to Grace, their connection to him put them in great danger. Would he try to *kill* them? And if he could look like any of the adults in Clawroot then there was no one to ask for help. All five of them were sitting ducks!

Another deep breath.

Grace had also said that the magic had chosen them for a reason and if they stayed together, they would be able to defeat him. Just like she had.

Riley's eyelids were finally starting to droop when movement in the corner of her eye caught her attention. She froze, then very slowly turned and peered into the darkness.

There, at the edge of the woods, a human figure was coming toward her. They moved cautiously, pausing every so often before moving forward again.

With light steps, Riley hurried to the edge of the porch and dropped down into the azalea bushes, making them rustle.

By the woods, the figure stood very still, their head tipped in Riley's direction. Riley held her breath and didn't move a muscle. Finally, the figure moved again, stepping out of the woods and into the light.

Riley almost gasped.

It was Aunt Alexis. The diffused light made her skin look ghostly pale. Her eyes were hooded with exhaustion and her mouth was carved into a stoic frown. She looked sick. Exactly how the Devourer should look, Riley thought.

All of the evidence pointed to Aunt Alexis. She had been at Wax & Wayne early on the day of the Full Moon Rite. The hunters' snare itself was deeply suspicious. Dhonielle had even told them that Aunt Alexis had gone back out that same night. She would have had plenty of time to find the young pups and steal Luke's wolf. Then there was the fact that she'd been the first adult to arrive after the attack on Milo. It all added up. Aunt Alexis had to be the Devourer in disguise.

Riley felt the truth clicking into place. But it didn't come with the kind of satisfaction she felt when she solved a puzzle. This felt terrible. She didn't want this to be true.

As she watched Aunt Alexis skulking into Clawroot, it suddenly occurred to her that all the young wolves were gathered in Cottonwood Hollow. What was the Devourer doing here?

Aunt Alexis crossed the yard and vanished around the side of the dining hall. Without a second of hesitation, Riley followed her into the dark.

Instantly, she knew something was wrong. The shadows deepened as if something had blotted out the moon and the hair on the back of Riley's neck prickled. Something was behind her. She could feel it. And she didn't want to turn around, but slowly, very slowly, she did.

At first she didn't see anything. Just the wall of trees where Aunt Alexis had stood a moment ago. Then her eyes landed on the bone-white arc of a massive tooth. She traced it up to find two yellow eyes with irises like crescent moons glimmering between the trees. From there, she found the shape of the beast. Its immense body curved through the forest like one long shadow, ending in a tail that crackled with lightning.

With a gulp, Riley dove into the azalea bushes around the dining hall, crouching on her knees in the dirt.

Step by step, the beast emerged from the forest, the scent of decaying leaves wafting ahead of its mouth. Riley's throat closed as first its teeth, then its eyes glided past her hiding place.

Its body came next. This close, it looked like a thunderstorm in the shape of a wolf. Clouds billowed in its belly and tumbled down each of its four legs, quivering with sparks of light as it crossed into Clawroot.

Riley spotted a band of silver glimmering around the wrist of the wolf's front left paw. A wolf cuff! No wonder the wards hadn't been broken. It *was* someone from the pack. It *was* someone they knew.

But it wasn't Aunt Alexis.

As the wolf turned toward the cabins at the edge of the stream, Riley's mind raced. *Luke! Milo!* What could

the Devourer possibly want from them when he'd already stolen their wolves?

But as Riley watched, the beast moved silently past the last cabin in the row, then the next, and the next. Until he reached cabin number three.

Panic jolted her into a run. The rest of her pack was asleep inside cabin three. Completely unaware that the Devouring Wolf was pressing his big yellow eye to the bedroom window.

Riley didn't know what she intended to do, but she knew that she had to try something. She ran until she had all but closed the gap between herself and the Devouring Wolf. Then she planted her feet, drew in a deep breath, and howled as hard as she had ever howled in her life.

To Riley's complete surprise, the Devourer stopped. A violent shudder moved through its body and it rounded on her with a snarl.

Riley stumbled back, hitting the ground with an "Oof!"

The Devourer wasted no time. The second Riley stopped howling, it lowered its head and charged.

28

LOCKED IN STONE

Riley didn't even have time to cry out before the wolf's head butted against her chest. She was thrown back, flying through the air. There was a brief sensation of wind against her cheeks. The clouds rolling far above her. She had just enough time to think about Aracely and how she didn't want to fly.

Ara—

She landed flat on her back.

Pain blossomed in her chest and behind her eyes. Her vision was speckled and uncertain. Where there should have been clouds or trees or grass there were endless stars.

Giant footsteps padded toward her. She had to move. But she could barely see! Riley blinked, fighting to clear her vision as she scrambled backward on hands and feet.

Slowly, the shape of the Devouring Wolf appeared before her. Its long, terrible teeth, its crescent-moon eyes, the burned smell of electricity.

Riley's back knocked into something hard. A wall. She'd made it all the way to one of the cabins and now she had nowhere to go. The Devourer was too close. She was trapped.

The wolf snarled and its body began to shimmer. The transformation swept smoothly from nose to tail, and before Riley's eyes the Devouring Wolf took on a human form Riley knew all too well.

Riley's mouth dropped open in horror.

Hazel eyes. A nose that bent just a little. Pale, wintery skin. Riley stared and stared at the face she'd seen every single day of her life. The Devourer bent and grabbed Riley by the shirt, hefting her into the air.

"Always in my way," said the creature wearing the face of Great Pack Leader Cecelia Callahan.

Riley couldn't think clearly. Her feet dangled in the air. Her mother's face was inches from her own. She'd been wrong wrong wrong, but she'd also been right. This was not her mother. But if that was true, then where was she?

"This time, at least, you've given me the perfect opportunity to get rid of you," said the Devourer.

Her mom's grip tightened. Riley struggled, kicking uselessly at the air.

"But you keep breaking the rules and going places you shouldn't." Mama C's eyes flashed. Yellow crescent moons sharpened around black pupils, and her teeth seemed to elongate when she smiled again. "You were bound to end up getting hurt."

The Devourer began to growl, a low, dark sound that echoed painfully in Riley's chest. With a shock, Riley realized it was acoustic magic.

Riley tried to scream, to howl, but no sound came out. She could feel the magic thrashing inside her, crushing her lungs from within.

"Riley!" a voice called, far away and thin.

The Devourer's growl grew louder, surrounding her like a cocoon.

"Riley! Help me!" the voice called again. This time Riley recognized it.

"Mom!" she cried. "Mama!"

Suddenly, the Devourer vanished, and Riley seemed to be standing in front of a massive stone. In the vision, it was webbed with crystalline veins that glittered and sparked, but there was something ominous about being this close. A tugging sensation that wanted Riley to come closer. No, not Riley. It wanted the Devourer. Wanted him to return to it.

Another growl sounded in Riley's mind, but beneath it, her mother's voice was urgent.

"Riley, listen to me. There is a stone in the woods that was hidden for a long time but isn't any longer. It's old magic—a prison that must always contain a prisoner. I didn't understand that when I found it and I let him out."

Riley shuddered in horror.

The stone had taken her mother.

She had been locked inside it for days while the Devourer roamed through the pack, stealing away the new wolves and gathering his strength.

"Mom," Riley gasped as the Devourer's magic pressed harder.

He was going to kill Riley. She would never get the chance to tell the others, to save Mama C, or tell Mama N how sorry she was. All they would know was that Riley had done exactly what Great Callahan had accused her of and put herself in danger by going out alone. Exactly what Grace had warned them against.

The Devourer would be unstoppable.

"Hang on, pup," Mama C said, speaking fast. "I can stall him, but I need you to run and get help. Tell the others where I am. I know you can find me again. I love you, Riley. Be strong. Be brave."

The Devourer snarled, and this time Riley felt the magic ripped away. It slashed through her like claws along a stone wall, tearing as the Devourer dragged it back.

Pain exploded inside Riley. She wasn't sure if she screamed or if it only felt like she screamed.

Riley! called four familiar voices.

Then a wave of darkness washed over her.

29

TRUST YOUR PACK

When Riley opened her eyes, Lydia was frowning at her. Riley blinked and tried again, but Lydia was still there and so was her frowning face.

The pain was also there, and Riley winced at the light glaring down from the ceiling.

"Dr. Khorram thought you'd have a headache," Lydia explained. She was seated on her own bed across from Riley. It looked like she'd been waiting for her to wake up. "He left you these painkillers if you want them."

On her bedside table were a glass of water and a little paper cup containing two orange pills. Riley tossed them back and chased them with a big swig of water.

They were alone in the bedroom. The air still smelled like jasmine from Aracely's soap. Judging from the light barreling through the windows, it was well past morning.

"What happened?" Riley asked in a raspy voice. Her brain felt like a squished grape.

"That's a good question." Lydia's mouth pinched in

disapproval. "We woke up in the middle of the night because you were screaming inside our heads. Do you know how terrifying that is?"

Memories of last night flooded in all at once. Aunt Alexis. The wolf. Mama C. The stone prison. Her heart started to pound, which made the pain in her head that much worse. Her mom was trapped inside the stone. She had to save her.

"You were also screaming for real," Lydia continued. "It woke up everyone in Clawroot. Ms. Montgomery, Luke, Bethany Books, even Dr. Khorram. We found you passed out on the ground. Your mom got to you first, which is just lucky, I guess."

Riley gaped at that. "Lucky?"

"You were in bad shape. Dr. Khorram checked you over and Great Callahan told us everything. Then we went to bed. Angry, I might add, which is something I really try to avoid."

Riley's brain finally caught up to everything that had happened. Cold sweat pricked along her neck. It was as if all the air had been sucked from her lungs. "Lydia," she whispered, grabbing on to her hands. "You don't understand. The Devouring Wolf. It's my mom!"

Lydia blinked. For a second Riley thought she hadn't heard her, then it all came crashing down. "Great Callahan? Are—are you sure?"

"I'm sure." Riley had never been so sure in all her life.

"Oh no." Lydia's eyes unfocused and she shook her head. "Oh no, no, no."

"What?" Riley demanded. "What is it?"

"She told us that she was out keeping watch and heard you scream. By the time she got to you, a wolf was running away, and you were on the ground."

A lie. But a believable one.

Lydia grew pale as she continued. "She said the wolf that attacked you was your Aunt Alexis. That the hunters' snare must have done more to her than we all thought to make her turn on her own like this. And the thing is, everyone believes it! We believed it!"

Riley looked across the room to the empty beds on the other side. Each one had been stripped, the quilts and sheets folded neatly and stacked at the foot. An uncomfortable sensation settled in Riley's chest at the sight.

"There's more," Lydia said.

Riley almost didn't want to ask. "What?"

"Dhonielle was really upset about her mom. I'm sure you can imagine. She was terrified and couldn't sleep all night, and first thing this morning, she left. With *your* mom."

Riley sprang out of bed. "Where did they go?"

"I don't know, but it's the middle of the day. She can't do anything to her now, can she? Everyone would see."

A part of Riley hoped that was true, but the rest of her was pretty certain it wasn't. She shook her head. "The Devourer knows who we are. Remember what Grace said. We can't let him separate us."

"Do you think he'd . . ." Lydia took a deep breath before continuing, "Kill her?"

"I won't let that happen," Riley said.

"We," said Lydia.

"What?"

"*We* won't let that happen." Lydia's frown had returned.

"Right, that's what I meant."

"Is it?" Lydia asked, eyes blazing. "Then why did you leave without us last night? Didn't you trust us enough to help you?"

Riley's cheeks warmed. "I didn't mean to, it just happened. I saw Aunt Alexis and I just followed her. I didn't really think about it."

"That's just it, Riley. You keep acting like you want to be an alpha. But if you want to be *our* alpha, then you have to think about us. You have to trust us enough to help you. Especially when things are dangerous."

Riley's stomach pitched. *Trust your pack.* Mama C always said it was the hardest rule and the most important. And Lydia was right. It didn't matter what her reasons were. She'd failed to do what leaders were supposed to do. She'd failed to trust the pack she had.

"I'm sorry," Riley said.

No sooner had she said the words than a terrified voice called in her mind, *Help!*

He nearly defeated us. When he got Annabeth alone, when he took her life, we thought all was lost. And it very nearly was.

You must not let him get you alone. Do not repeat our mistakes. You must trust each other and stay together. No matter what, stay together.

30

YOUR STRENGTH AND TRUE POWER . . .

Dhonielle! Riley's stomach plunged. The Devourer had waltzed right into their cabin and taken Dhonielle.

"Did you guys hear that?!" Aracely burst into the room curls-first. Behind her, Kenver followed, dressed in a slick black button-down and gray plaid pants.

"We heard it," Lydia confirmed. "The Devourer has her."

"Teeth and claws," Aracely groaned. "How do you know?"

"Because the Devourer is pretending to be my mom." It was surprisingly easy to say even if it reminded Riley that her real mom was trapped inside the stone prison.

"She feels far away," Kenver said, eyes closed. "It's too hard to hear her anymore."

Riley realized that Kenver was right. Wherever Dhonielle was, she was getting farther away.

"Everyone, close your eyes. If we can dream together and hear each other's thoughts, then we can reach Dhonielle."

They joined hands and stood in a circle with their eyes closed.

Riley fixed an image of her cousin in her mind. She imagined her warm brown cheeks, the twin braids that flipped out behind her ears; she imagined the hunch of her shoulders and the way she always looked like something was about to fall on top of her.

She pictured her as perfectly as she could and then she held her there in her mind until . . .

Help!

The voice was small and distant. Scared.

Help me!

The image in Riley's mind was replaced by one of Dhonielle huddled inside the husk of an ancient cottonwood tree. She clutched a lithocharm to her chest, letting it deepen the shadows in her hiding place. In addition to the image, Riley felt a strong sense of direction. It was as if she would be able to find Dhonielle even if her eyes were shut.

Dhonielle! Riley called. *We're coming!*

All four of them opened their eyes together. Without speaking a word, they hurried from the cabin and ran

straight for the woods. They didn't need to share directions because they were all following that feeling of connection. To each other and to Dhonielle.

It's Aunt CeCe. Dhonielle's voice was a whisper. *She's
the Devouring Wolf.*

We know, Riley assured her. *She tried to hurt me last
night. Are you okay?*

*I'm fine. I should have noticed right away that something
was wrong, but I was so upset. As soon as I realized I didn't
know where we were, I ran, but . . . I still don't know where
I am.* Dhonielle sounded embarrassed to admit this. *He's
still out there. I know he's just waiting for me to move.*

Stay put. We're coming to you! Kenver called.

"Hey!" Aracely stopped them at the edge of the woods.
"Shouldn't we go get some help?"

Riley looked back at Clawroot. There were plenty of people here. Plenty of adults who were supposed to be the ones that handled giant problems like
this. It was what Mama C had told her to do. But who
would believe that the person they all thought to be
Cecelia Callahan was actually the Devouring Wolf?

The truth of that hit Riley all at once. Great Callahan
was in charge of nearly everything. It had been Great
Callahan who suggested that a hunter was responsible
for stealing the wolves of Luke, Milo, and the others, Great
Callahan who organized the search. It had been
Great Callahan who shut Riley down in front of everyone

when she said it was the Devouring Wolf. It had always been Great Callahan.

And there was no one left in Clawroot who would believe otherwise.

Dhonielle was in trouble, the real Cecelia Callahan was trapped inside the Devourer's stone, and the four of them were completely on their own.

"It's up to us," Riley said.

"But what are we going to do?!" Aracely shouted. "Go out there and ask him politely to stop?"

Riley tried to clear her head. Aracely wasn't wrong. Riley needed a plan. She needed to be brave enough to do the tough stuff, to encourage the others, and act like a leader. But most of all, she needed to trust her pack.

"We aren't going to Dhonielle!" The idea burst in Riley's head like a firework had gone off.

"Why not?" Lydia asked.

"Because we need her to come to us." Riley started walking again as she explained, "My mom is trapped and needs our help. The stone they used to bind the Devourer has her now, which means the stone still works, it's just holding the wrong person."

"Then how did he get out in the first place?" Lydia asked.

"Maybe it was the ringward," Kenver explained. "Grace said that they placed him inside a stone, and they surrounded that stone with a ringward to prevent anyone from finding it. Maybe something happened to break the ward."

"What kind of something?" Aracely sounded even more alarmed.

"It could have been something natural like an earth-quake," Kenver said.

"In Kansas?" Aracely asked.

"Or it could have been something magical. Like a hunter. Or a witch." Kenver didn't sound happy about this option. "A very powerful witch."

"But who would let the Devourer out on purpose?" Lydia asked. "And why?"

Kenver didn't answer. No one did, but they were all thinking the same thing: if someone did this on purpose, then there was something even worse than the Devourer out there.

"Whatever it was doesn't matter right now," Riley said definitively. "We need to free my mom from the stone, then bind the Devourer inside it again. Exactly how Grace Barley said."

"But how will we find the stone?" Kenver asked.

"I can find it." Riley hadn't even had a chance to tell them about last night. About the vision she'd had when the Devourer attacked her, and her mom's instructions. But she trusted them to trust her, and she could explain it all later. "Just follow me."

The clouds that had moved in the previous day had

grown even thicker. Thunder rumbled overhead and the forest came alive with a hissing rain. Soon, the ground grew slick with mud, slowing them down, but they kept running.

Dhonielle, she called. *Change of plans! We need you to come to us.*

What? No! Dhonielle's voice squeaked. *He'll get me!*

Riley hesitated. For this to work, they needed to find a way to lead the Devourer to the stone, but Dhonielle was afraid and she wasn't a fast runner. It was a bad combination.

"I'll go help her," Lydia said. "I'll create a distraction so she can get a head start, and then we'll lead him straight to you."

Lydia was doing it again. She was jumping in and volunteering to do the tough stuff while Riley was working on the plan. Only this time, Riley didn't mind. It felt like they were in sync with each other, Lydia anticipating her needs before she'd said them aloud. It was exactly how a pack should work.

She wanted to reach out and squeeze Lydia's hand, but instead she said, "Be careful."

"See you soon." Lydia broke away from the three of them, hurrying toward Dhonielle and the Devouring Wolf.

It was strange to be able to feel both Dhonielle and Lydia, to know where they were even if they were still some distance away. Riley felt their connection like a web spread out between them, thin cords of magic tying them all together.

Soon the rain died down and they could see again. Just ahead, the trees thinned around a grove—the same grove from Riley's vision, with one difference: there was no giant stone in sight.

There were small rocks everywhere. But none were larger than the ones they'd moved from the Stone Pool.

"Are you sure this is the place?" Aracely asked, confused.

"This is it." Riley searched the clearing a second and third time, but there was still no stone. "He—he must have moved it."

"Where?" Kenver asked.

Riley tried to think. Tried to come up with the answer. She'd just seen it last night. He hadn't had time to take it very far and still get back to trick Dhonielle. If he'd moved it, it had to be close.

Her eyes fell again on the small stones dotting the clearing, emerging from the dirt like the tips of tiny icebergs.

"The rocks!" There was one way to move a rock without moving it at all. "He buried it! One of these is the stone!"

"Oooh, easy!" Aracely chirped. "Like stealing kisses from a puppy."

"Spread out!" Kenver was already running to the farthest edge of the field.

Riley tried to count up all the rocks she could see. There were dozens, and the ground was smooth and undisturbed around each. Of course, someone as powerful as the Devouring Wolf could ease the stone into the ground the same way Riley had eased a grape inside a rock.

They just needed time to figure out which one was the prison.

We're coming! Lydia's voice was breathless.

But time was something they didn't have.

Riley spun toward the others. Dhonielle and Lydia were close and moving fast. She could feel it along with the rapid beating of her own heart. They didn't have time to search this whole field.

"Keep looking!" Riley shouted. "Look for one that's dark granite with silver veins."

She swept her gaze from stone to stone, hoping that at any moment she would find the right one.

"I'm not finding it!" Aracely shouted from across the field.

"Me neither," Kenver answered.

It had to be here. It simply had to be here.

Riley! The voice stopped her in her tracks.

Mom!

It was close. Only a few feet from where Riley stood. She hurried toward it, calling again, *Mom! Mama!* And then she saw it.

A rock unlike the others, with crystalline veins that glittered darkly against gray stone.

He's right on top of us! Dhonielle shrieked as she and Lydia sprinted into the clearing. There was mud on their faces and in their hair. Their eyes were wide with terror, and every breath they took was harsh.

Hard on their heels was the beast. His body taller and more massive than Riley remembered.

"Aracely! Kenver!" Riley shouted. "It's here!"

Riley spun in time to see Dhonielle crash to her knees. Lydia caught her hand and dragged her back to her feet, but they weren't fast enough. The Devourer opened his jaws wide, ready to clamp them down on their small bodies.

Riley raced forward on instinct.

"Devourer!" she shouted. "I have a message for you from Grace Barley!"

The Devourer stopped and swiveled its massive head in Riley's direction. Yellow crescent-moon eyes pinned her in place. She felt her heart tap-tap-tapping against her ribs, her blood whispering in her ears.

Riley. Lydia sounded like she wanted to tell her to run. But running wasn't an option anymore.

Free the stone, she told the group. *I'll distract him. Just free the stone.*

A tremor moved through Riley's legs as the Devourer took a step in her direction.

In her peripheral vision, she could see Lydia and Dhonielle helping Aracely and Kenver with the stone. Lifting just as they had at the Stone Pool.

The Devourer snarled. Lightning crackled through his stormy body and a gust of wet breath engulfed Riley. Then he roared.

The sound vibrated through her, wrapped around her like a fist, and squeezed all the breath from her lungs.

At first Riley could do nothing but brace herself against it. Then she took a gulp of foul-smelling air and roared right back.

She leaned in, her small face nose-to-nose with the Devouring Wolf. Her own roar swallowed by his massive growl.

It wasn't working.

She was nothing but a pebble in a swift-running stream, all but useless against the current.

The Devourer darted forward then, and that sinister stormy magic coiled around Riley once more. Lifting her into the air as it had before. Plunging into her.

Pain expanded her chest, ripping and twisting like fire. In that moment, she felt the wolf inside her. Her wolf. It had been there all along. Rooted so deeply in her magic that it could never be stolen away.

But as the Devourer's magic tore through her, she could feel those roots breaking one by one.

The wolf that lived inside her was being devoured.

31

. . . IS EACH OTHER

Then four howls surrounded Riley. They rushed over her shoulders and around her legs, sliding between her and the Devourer like a shield and protecting her from his terrible magic. He snarled and tightened his grip.

"Kenver, now!" Lydia shouted.

Riley could only dimly see as Kenver bent and scooped up two handfuls of mud. She had just enough time to squeeze her own eyes shut as Kenver's hands glowed softly, transforming the mud to dust. Then they tossed it at the Devouring Wolf. Straight into his eyes.

The Devourer scrambled back, blinking furiously and releasing Riley.

She fell through the air, but before she hit the ground, a howl slipped beneath her and caught her. She landed neatly on her feet.

"Thanks, Dhonielle," she said with a smile for her cousin. The pain in her chest twisted sharply, but there was no time to rest. "Now!" she shouted.

Five howls rose together, braiding around one another in a perfect harmony of sound.

The Devouring Wolf ground to a halt. He shivered, shuddered, and stooped beneath the force of their call. Their combined magic was too much for him to resist.

Several yards away, the stone stood ready. Thanks to Grace and her diary, Riley knew exactly what they needed to do.

Riley linked arms with Lydia on one side and Dhonielle on the other, who then linked arms with Aracely and Kenver. Together, they moved forward, driving the Devourer backward with their howl one step at a time. They were the key; they would unlock the stone and bind him within it.

The Devourer snarled, but real fear painted his features.

It was working.

Gradually, slowly, they pushed him ever closer to the stone until he was only a step away.

Behind him, the glittery veins began to pulse and glow as though it wasn't a stone, but a gray heart.

The Devourer twisted, trying to avoid the stone, but his tail brushed the surface. His heels hit the stone a second later and . . .

Nothing happened.

Lydia gasped, Kenver scowled, and Dhonielle muttered, "Oh no."

"It's not working," Aracely whispered.

"Keep howling!" Riley shouted.

A shimmer moved down the Devourer's body as he transformed into a man with silver-and-black hair. His mouth was set in a terrible sneer and he focused pale blue eyes on Riley. He raised one hand and placed it against the stone, stroking it as though it were a pet.

"If you ever want to see your mother alive again, you'll stop making that noise," he said in a voice that was smooth and cold.

They stopped howling.

"There is no need to fight," he added. "That is something Grace Barley and the others never understood. All you have to do is help me break the room inside that stone and I'll leave." A sharp smile sliced across his face. "You'll never see me again. I'll leave you alone and take my revenge on the hunters who killed my family."

Riley shook her head. "You steal wolves that don't belong do you. We can't let you do that."

"Let me?" His features contorted into a mask of incredulity. "But, my dear, you must. I am doing this for you, for all wolves. You have no idea what waits out there, beyond this precious pack of yours. You have no idea how much evil lurks in the hearts of hunters and witches." He spat the last word. "What they did to me was beyond my control. But what I will do to them will not be."

"Are you saying you think stealing wolves is justified?!" Aracely shouted, but even she sounded scared.

"A means to an end." The Devourer shrugged. "Your darling Great Callahan thinks it's enough to keep to yourselves and protect your borders, but that is egregiously naive. One way or another, she is going to get you all killed, your pretty wolf heads stuffed and mounted on a wall, your teeth polished and strung like beads on a necklace."

The image was so gruesome that Riley couldn't help but shiver.

"You're wrong." Riley balled her fingers into fists, but she didn't know what to do. She was out of ideas. "We won't help you!"

The Devourer took a step forward and turned his terrible eyes on Dhonielle.

"Stand against me and I will haunt you for the rest of your life. I will always be waiting to pull you down!" Dhonielle trembled as he turned next to Lydia. "I will kill everyone who loves you." His eyes leapt to Kenver. "If anyone even does."

"You think you're a pack?" His features morphed into those of Cecelia Callahan once more, his voice becoming the same one Riley had heard every day of her life when it said, "You're not even a real wolf."

The words *not a real wolf* hissed through her head, venomous and cruel. Riley's fingers went numb. The Devourer was so much stronger than they were. This was a wolf who had survived decades locked in stone. Who had stolen the wolves of his own prime pack. What hope could five twelve-year-old kids have against someone like him?

Somehow she'd convinced herself that this was the right thing to do, but she'd been wrong.

The Devourer grinned and turned next to Aracely.

"You are last for a reason. You are—"

Aracely didn't give him a chance to respond. She pelted him with a lithocharm right between the eyes, stunning him to silence. The Devourer stumbled back with a cry of outrage.

"You'd be cooler if you were an actual fossil!" Aracely shouted.

And suddenly Riley knew what to do. The Devourer had said it himself: there was a room inside that stone.

Dhonielle, Lydia, you two keep him here! she said.

They nodded and pelted the Devourer with a howl that forced him back against the stone.

Follow me! Riley told the others, spinning on her heel and racing around the stone. *We have to call him through the stone. We can't just push him inside, because there's no room. We have to draw my mom out and pull him in at the same time.*

Together, they raised their hands, holding them an inch away from the stone's surface.

How does this work? Aracely asked.

Riley took a deep breath and tried to quash the fear trembling in her lungs. This was just like the grape. Only instead of a fruit inside a rock, it was her mom. *Envision the room inside the stone. Envision Great Callahan inside it and then call her out.*

This time their voices were soft and steady, bending and weaving like three bands of silver. Riley pictured her mother inside the stone, she pictured their call coiling around her, and then she pictured pulling her out.

Something stirred beneath the glittering surface. A face or a hand. Something was coming toward them.

It's working! Lydia called just as a great howl rose from the other side of the stone. The Devourer shrieked in pain as he was slowly pulled inside it.

The last thing they heard was his voice promising, "I will come for you one day, little wolves."

Then, in a blistering flash of light, he was gone. On the other side of the stone, Cecelia Callahan collapsed on the ground.

"Mom!" Riley exclaimed, rushing forward to help her mom to her feet.

Mama C exhaled slowly, blinking at the sudden light. Then, she reached for her daughter and held Riley in the most perfect hug there ever was. "It *was* you. Oh, my brave, brave pup. You found me."

Every emotion Riley had ever felt was suddenly in her throat, preventing her from speaking.

Instead she nodded and squeezed a little harder.

32

BACK TO NORMAL . . . ALMOST

The mood in Clawroot had changed by the time they made it back.

A small group had gathered around the porch of cabin six and everyone was chatting happily. In the middle stood three figures: Luke, Paislee, and Milo.

"Mom! Ri!" Milo threw himself toward them. "They're back! Our wolves are all back! Whoa, do you know that you're both covered in mud?"

Mama C laughed and pulled Milo into her arms. "Don't worry, I'm happy to share with you."

"Mmffff," said Milo.

Riley felt a brief surge of hope. Maybe something had shifted inside her, too, and she'd just been too distracted to notice. Maybe she and the others would transform into wolves now. But just as quickly as the thought had occurred, it was gone again. Nothing had changed. She could feel it. She was the same tenderfoot pup she'd been yesterday. Somehow, though, that was okay.

"I don't know what you did, but I know you did something." Luke appeared next to Riley with Paislee Scott at his side. "Thank you."

Riley shrugged and said, "I'm glad you got your wolves back."

Bethany Books's voice rose above the crowd, calling them all to attention. "All right, pups, we need to get you back into wolf form. Your magic is still developing! So follow me, please."

Luke, Paislee, Milo, and the others followed Bethany. They closed their eyes and listened as she guided them through their first intentional transformation.

It started slowly. A shimmer moved over their skin like a pale shadow, like ripples on the surface of a pool. Then their bodies coiled down like little fern fronds reaching for the earth, their necks stretched long with powerful muscles, and fur danced down their spines.

Riley watched with a little envy as Milo shook out his coat. It was a deep earthy brown with white that dusted his belly and forepaws. He made a really good wolf.

Then they were gone, racing into the woods to meet up with the rest of the pack and let their magic grow and mature as it should.

• • •

An hour later, the five of them were in cabin three snacking on fruit juice and crackers prescribed by Dr. Khorram while they waited for their parents.

Mama N arrived looking frantic. Her hair was fraying out of its braid as though she'd spent the drive here pushing her hands through it repeatedly.

"Riley," she gasped, sweeping her into her arms.

Riley hugged her back for a long time. So much had happened since she'd left the house in a huff, but it felt like just yesterday they'd been shouting at one another.

"Mama N," Riley said when she finally pulled away. "I'm really sorry."

A little frown creased Mama N's brow. "For what?"

"For saying what I said. About wanting to be a real wolf." Riley thought about all the times she'd worried about not being a real wolf. About finding herself without a pack, without people who would care about her no matter what. In the end, it wasn't the transformation that made her a real wolf. It wasn't anything about her body, in fact. What made her a wolf was her pack. "I know that you're a real wolf. And so am I."

Mama N smiled sadly and cupped Riley's cheek in the palm of her hand. "Yes, you are."

Tears welled in Riley's eyes. A few days ago, she wouldn't have believed it. Now, looking around at Lydia and Aracely, Kenver and Dhonielle, she knew without a doubt that it was one hundred percent true.

"Is it okay if we stay out here for a few more days?"

Mama N looked to the other parents. Uncle Will looked like he might never let go of Dhonielle again, Aracely's sisters were clustered around her like plumage, Lydia's uncles were barely keeping it together, and Kenver's mom hadn't stopped crying.

"I promise we won't leave Clawroot without telling anyone." Riley looked at the others and knew they felt the same way she did. In spite of all that had happened, they weren't ready to leave.

"Well, if it's okay with the others." Mama N sounded reluctant but willing.

One by one, the other parents agreed, and after an evening of many, many questions and the biggest dinner Riley could remember ever eating, they were allowed to return to their cabin together. Everything felt better, even if they didn't have all the answers.

Just before lights-out there was a knock on the door. Riley's mom entered, looking a bit better than she had earlier in the day. She'd had a shower and changed into fresh clothes and looked much more like Great Callahan than Mama C.

"I thought you all might have a few more questions for me," she said, folding her hands in front of her. It was such a familiar gesture. One Riley was certain she hadn't seen her make since the Full Moon Rite. How many other clues had she missed?

"Aunt CeCe," Dhonielle started. "Is he gone for good?"

"He is locked up again and this time we know exactly where he is. The ringwards they used last time were a little too good. They hid the stone even from us, which might have been their intention. I'm sure they didn't expect them to fail." Mama C spoke to them openly, honestly, and not at all like they were children.

"Why did they fail?" Kenver asked.

Mama C hesitated, but after a brief pause, she continued. "We aren't sure. It looks like someone tampered with them. If we'd known they were there, we could have taken better precautions. That's why we don't keep secrets like this. We write them down, pass them to the next generation. The pack a hundred years from now is still our pack."

"But if you think a person did this, isn't there a chance he could get out again?" Dhonielle asked, shoulders hunching up around her ears.

Mama C only said, "Try not to worry."

Aracely cracked a grin. "Have you met her? The only thing she likes more than worrying is reading!"

That made Dhonielle smile.

"But we're safe again?" Kenver asked.

"Thanks to you five," Mama C confirmed. "All the

stolen wolves have been returned, including my own. For which I am very grateful."

Everything had gone back normal. Everything except for one.

"What about us?" Riley asked. "If it was the Devouring Wolf's release that kept us from shifting, why haven't we heard the call?"

They'd scoured Grace Barley's diary for any hint of whether or not her pack had transformed after trapping the Devouring Wolf, but there was none.

A quick frown flashed across Mama C's face. "The hard truth is that we don't know. We're going to put a few calls out to the other packs to see if there's more in other histories, but this may take some time to unravel."

Riley felt her heart grow heavy and a refrain echoed in the far distance of her mind: *Not a real wolf.* She wondered what people would think of her if she never transformed. What Stacey would think.

She looked at her friends. In their faces she could see the same shadow of disappointment. They all wanted to know what it felt like for their bodies to transform. They wanted to run through the woods with magic tingling between their toes.

But as Riley looked from one to the other, she also knew that they'd found something just as important.

"It's okay," she said. "We've found our pack."

EPILOGUE

THE FIRST FULL MOON OF WINTER

It was the first full moon of winter, and in five separate homes, five tenderfoot wolves were each preparing for bed.

One sat alone in her bedroom, her nose deep in a book while her mom called up a ten-minute warning to lights-out that she didn't hear.

One had pushed her journal aside in favor of her laptop, where she was studying new recipes for candy and tarts.

Another was listening to music, her feet keeping time with the rhythm while her sisters argued over the bathroom.

One sat across the kitchen table from their parents, scowling at a puzzle that was only shades of blue.

And yet another sat with her window open in spite of the colder temperatures, surrounded by cats.

It was the first full moon of winter and an early snow was on the way, but so, too, was something else.

Wolf magic is not caused by full moons any more than it is caused by a heavy rainstorm or a comet passing by. But wolf magic always seeks balance. Now that the danger of the woods had passed, something new was coming. Something that called to the wolves waiting inside the five young pups.

It surprised them at first. They'd gone so long without a transformation that none of them were expecting it. When they heard a faraway howl coming from somewhere outside, they nearly ignored it.

But the call continued. Crooning in the distance, a single, perfect note cast against the silence of the night. It was quiet yet unmistakable. The call of First Wolf.

One by one, each of them paused what they were doing and moved toward a window or a door to listen harder.

They asked, "Do you hear that?" but no one in their homes did.

It was a delicate, urgent note. One only the five of them could hear. And one by one, each of them understood.

It was the first full moon of winter, and it was finally time.

ACKNOWLEDGMENTS

The idea for this book took shape on a long walk with my wife down a narrow strip of the Gulf Coast. It was winter and I was foolishly walking through the surf, letting the cold water rush over my feet as I tossed ideas out one after another. I was eager to write for younger audiences but hadn't yet found the idea that felt like a personal treasure. Until the words "queer werewolf packs" came out of my mouth.

My wife, who is never excited about ideas until they've taken shape, gave me a brief nod of her head, and that was all the encouragement I needed. So, first and foremost, thank you to Tessa Gratton, for nodding when I needed a nod and telling me to quit walking in frigid waters before I froze my feet off. Good advice then and now.

I am grateful to my agent, Lara Perkins, for helping to shape this book and find it a beautiful home at Razorbill; to my editors there, Ruta Rimas, Simone Roberts-Payne, Gretchen Durning, and Chris Hernandez, for finding all the ways it could improve still; to the incredible team of managing editors and copyeditors, Jayne Ziemba, Sola

Akinlana, Abigail Powers, Delia Davis, Marinda Valenti, Krista Ahlberg, Kellie Hultgren, and Kristy Gilbert for their enviable attention to detail; to the designers, Jess Jenkins and Tony Sahara, for creating exquisite packaging; to the artists, Karl Kwasny and Tyler Champion, for indelible illustrations; and to all the people who worked on this project and whose names I don't know: thank you.

A small collection of readers were crucial to the forming of this book and I am indebted to each of them. To Amanda Sellet, who read more than once and offered hilarious insights on werewolf puberty; to Justina Ireland, who came in at a critical moment and pointed out exactly what I was doing wrong; to Julie Murphy, who suggested the inclusion of pages from Grace Barley's diary, many, many thanks.

I'm also grateful to my friends, who are just generally the best, but a few in particular made this book a little extra special. Thank you to Dhonielle Clayton, Zoraida Córdova, Lydia Ash, Adib Khorram, and Bethany Hagen for lending me their names in the creation of this cast.

My family is always a source of joy and support, and I'm especially grateful to my nieces, who asked for all the details about this book and told me it was good but woefully short on pictures. Hopefully they'll read it anyway.

And finally, my wife again, because she is with me every step of the way. Even when I walk in the winter sea.

DISCARD
MT. PLEASANT